PAPER SOULS

ALLIE BURKE

Booktrope Editions
Seattle WA 2014

Cover Design by Shari Ryan

Edited by Katrina M. Randall

This is a work of fiction. Names, characters, places, brands, media, and incidents are either the product of the author's imagination or are used fictitiously. Any resemblance to similarly named places or to persons living or deceased is unintentional.

Print ISBN 978-1-62015-483-0

EPUB ISBN 978-1-62015-493-9

Library of Congress Control Number: 2014915989

For B and Comrade,
and for Fray-Fray.
Danke.

"I find hope in the darkest of days, and focus in the brightest. I do not judge the universe." –Dalai Lama

ACKNOWLEDGMENTS

I would like to thank all the people in the universe who inspired this story, especially the evil ones. To Schizophrenia for lighting the way through years of psychosis: thank you. *Paper Souls* wouldn't be *Paper Souls* without you.

To all the wonderful people at Booktrope, who believe firsthand in the art of literature, thank you. Katherine Fye Sears, for your attention to a book that was more important to me than anything I've ever written. Ken Shear, because you are totally awesome. My lovely editor, Katrina Mendolera, for nodding with a smile when the words 'artistic choice' actually came out of my mouth. Tess Thompson and Jayme Nimick for the late (and early) conversations about said artistic choices. Thank the universe we had wine. My book manager, Penelope Brown, who, even having been invited late to the game, made a fearless leap without thinking twice about it. Ally Bishop, for the absolutely stunning interview and everything that you do for authors every day; and Shari Ryan, for the gorgeous cover that we basically fought wars to get right. Big thanks to Stefan Sharkanski and Tiffani Velez for your most amazing counsel on the Russian language.

Jesse James, you once told me that I had made art and had created immortality by doing so. You sir, have created immortality in me, because you have touched my life in ways that had always been impossible for someone like me, and I will remember that, and you, forever.

Marni Mann, whose book, whose friendship, whose love, pushed me to finish this stupid fucking book. I cannot count the times I told myself that I couldn't do it, I couldn't write this, it was too painful, I wasn't a good enough writer, blah blah blah, nobody cares. Marni Mann,

I wrote this book for you. I mean, I wrote this book for me, and for so many things, but ultimately, I wrote this book for you, too, because I wouldn't have been able to bear it if you were disappointed that it never got finished. You were with me every step of the way, and I just wanted to write a book half as good as *Memoirs*. I want you to know that it wouldn't exist without you.

I am grateful for people like Hazel Godwin at Craves the Angst, who made everyone I know excited about this book long before I was excited about this book.

Alfredo Gutierrez, for vogue fashion shows in the middle of bars, inappropriate cartoons, Burberry car seats, and sociopathic masturbation: you have become one of the most constant elements in my universe and have saved me from myself more than once. I am so happy to have you in my life.

To all the lovely people in my aura who don't give a shit about books, but give a shit about *my* books: that's kind of why we're friends. Thank you.

To all who have expressed an interest in this book, namely, my loyal readers, thank you. It is important to me because it is important to Schizophrenia and I will be forever grateful to you for your willingness to be a part of it.

PROLOGUE

IT'S HARD TO REMEMBER THINGS.

The most important things, the experiences that leave marks on our souls for everyone to see, those marks that reflect our most intense emotions in a glass pane, we will never forget.

But we don't remember everything. People call it human nature; nobody is perfect, etcetera.

What is perfect, really? The absence of perfection and the existence of human nature in place of something we want to do or we don't want to do, is an excuse, not an exoneration.

That was the thing about telling a story. The universe requires balance. Nothing, *nothing*, can exist without it. There is no life, no light, without death, without darkness.

There is no memory without emptiness.

CHAPTER ONE

EMILY'S DOOR KNOCKED. Or, rather, someone knocked on Emily's door. She pressed the button on the side of her new phone, illuminating the giant screen. It was after two in the morning, and phones were big now.

She looked around at the belongings that seemed to be the epitome of some distant life, as if they didn't belong to her. She had returned home just three days before. She hadn't seen him in so long, and currently, she, and her entire life, was a mess.

He knocked again.

Once upon a time, she would have run to the closest mirror to ensure her appearance was appropriate. Appropriate meaning perfect.

The ideal of external perfection seemed so mundane to her now.

She opened the door.

He charged at her, squeezing her hips so hard that, as he kissed her, she knew they would eventually bruise.

Emily liked it. He knew that.

His hand glided around to the small of her back, sailing up her spine, his fingernails painting trails of red through her shirt onto her pale skin. He seized the back of her neck while his other hand cupped her ass, lifting her against the back of the front door. The weight of his contoured body held her there while he unbuttoned his jeans. With the tips of her toes, Emily reached up to his waist and pushed his pants down to his ankles. He clenched the edge of her dress between his callused fingertips, lifting it up and pushing her cotton underwear to the side. He entered her imprudently, without caution.

She gasped, and a breath escaped his wickedly erotic smile.

He slowed, and her warmth began to drip down his legs. He paused.

Emily didn't look deep into his eyes or any stupid, epical gesture of humanity-defining love, or anything like that. It was all bullshit: true love, soul mates, all of it. You fall in love and you fall out of love and you fall in love again. A hundred times over the course of your lifetime. Humans were never meant to be with just one person. Unless you were Adam and Eve. Which was bullshit too, obviously.

She just waited.

His hand slipped under the back of her dress and he unclutched her bra with two fingers. They always used to joke about his experience with bras. If he couldn't get it unhooked in two seconds or less, it was defective.

The upper portion of Emily's skull echoed as it popped against the back of the door. Her right nipple was between his thumb and forefinger. The sensation bordered between euphoric and unbearable as he squeezed, while jamming his stiffness inside her. Her legs began to tremble as he slowed to a melodic rhythm. He clutched her thighs and wrapped them around his waist. The trembling stopped only for a moment, until he wrapped his fingers around her neck, hard enough to invoke a reaction, but not so that he would leave a mark. He squeezed, and his hand trailed down her chest—painting lines that matched the ones on her back—over her flat stomach, stopping just short of the spot that connected them at present. He kissed her neck, biting down ever so gently. He just wasn't that guy. He'd never leave a mark where it could be seen. He didn't need to mark his territory like a fucking dog.

Emily's breath stuck in her chest as the warmth between her legs caught on fire.

You missed me, he whispered, his words barely comprehensible to her.

Please be quiet, Emily said.

Okay, he said.

Emily's spine dug into the door. His presence drowned her: her nipples were tender, her thighs the shade of yellow that preemptively indicated bruising. Her skin bore the lines of a sketch artist's canvas. He was everywhere.

Yes, he groaned. *Yes.*

Emily used to scream in bed with men and with him, at first. Like a stupid little girl.

Now, Emily didn't make a sound. There was something more defining about the soundless reality that condemned the paradigm of passion. Only the thick scent of breathless sex filled her house.

He collapsed to his knees, the strength of his upper body bringing her down with him, and her eagerness pushed him backwards so he lay on his back on the carpeted floor. She pressed her palms onto his hairy chest and, disregarding whatever it was that he may or may not have wanted, Emily made her own music with their rhythm, releasing the rapture of her being so many times that it spilled down his sides and onto the plush below. Effortlessly, he lifted her from him as he finished and his own bound with hers as it rained down onto his skin.

He looked at her in that way. That way that, when Emily used to look back at the memory of it, she would cry. The same memory that made her smile now.

It was like that the next four times they found themselves entangled in one another before noon the next day, in between shifts of half-dreamt sleep.

It was always like that.

But that was just Brendan and Emily. Two people who simultaneously loved one another too much and not enough.

Insanity is defined by repeating the same act while expecting a different result.

Schizophrenia made insanity easy on Emily, though. Love is like a shadow. You see it right in front of your eyes, but it isn't really there.

Is it?

She looked around at the home that had been hers for years and let her throat attempt to suck down the lump that was stuck in it. The pipe dream that had been her future hours before was just that. Her heart began to pound as shadows enveloped her existence.

She couldn't stay here. She'd be in prison in an hour.

There was only one place she had left to go where she wouldn't disappear forever. If she was completely honest with herself, there was no other place she would rather be, anyway. Now, or ever.

THREE YEARS EARLIER

CHAPTER TWO

EMILY CLOSED HER EYES once again in an effort to allow more tears to fall. She couldn't see through the film of sorrow building up in front of her eyes. They would dry up on her cheeks eventually, like the others had.

She tuned out the mother-of-two next to her, who was babbling about how depression wasn't so bad, and they had really good doctors here, and they care because they actually have medical doctors and not just psychiatrists, and therapists, and who fucking cares.

Emily wasn't depressed. She was crazy. There is a difference, apparently.

She lay in a twin bed with gray sheets. Next to the bed there was an old wood box with a drawer, which could have been defined as a dresser, maybe. She wasn't sure of its purpose since they had confiscated her purse, which contained her cell phone and the only book she had with her.

If she wanted to kill herself before she got in here, she really wanted to do some damage now.

You have children? Emily asked the woman lying in the bed on the other side of the room, catching a snippet of her incessant babble.

Yes, the woman answered. Two girls.

She didn't have any makeup on and there was a glow under her droopy eyes. Her blonde hair was dull, yet Emily thought her oddly stunning. There was a certain beauty about a bare woman who could actually pull it off. Not that she had a choice. Emily would be free of makeup for some indeterminable amount of time once she washed her face. If they had luxuries like soap here, that is.

That must be really tough on you and your husband, Emily said.
It's not so bad, the woman replied. I've only been here six weeks.
Emily stared at the white wall beyond the foot of her bed. Only six
weeks. Yeah. She was definitely going to off herself the first chance
she got.

She wasn't trying to escape anything, like maybe this woman was.
There was nothing necessarily terrible to escape. She had an apartment
and a car and a boyfriend and she owned her own business. She was
only twenty-five. What else could she possibly want?

But she had been in her car, after months of doctors and pills and
talking, so much talking. Brendan had once told her that he wished he
knew of a way to shut himself up, to make himself stop talking forever.
Emily knew how to shut him up. All you had to do was graze the tips of
your fingertips over Brendan's skin to get him to stop talking. Preferably
his back, starting at the edge of his hairline and traveling down his spine.
Fingers were feathers and skin was air. The essence of that defining
connection would shut everyone up, and the whole world would stop
talking. Of course, that would only be beneficial to Brendan if Emily
was there; because she didn't think too many people knew that about
him. And Emily wasn't there very often, so Brendan would have no
choice other than to keep on talking. Forever. Just like she had to keep
talking, since she didn't have a magical shut off switch like he did.
Emily hadn't seen a therapist, but each specialist she was recommended
to see wanted to know why she was there. And then she had to explain
it again: her life story, why she couldn't sleep, what she saw, what she
heard, what she didn't hear, etcetera. She'd experimented with more than
five different prescription drugs in the last two months alone. First it
was, I'm sorry you've had such a hard life, then, you see things because
you can't sleep, then, mild Schizoaffective Disorder, to, oh, yeah, you
have Paranoid Schizophrenia. Interesting how they got there. She wished
they would have just come out with it to start with.

Emily Colt, you are a raving lunatic.

She would have been totally fine with that diagnosis.

But she had been in the car. She couldn't remember if she had taken
her medication today; she was not consistent with it and had been off
it in the last months as many times as she had been on it. Out of nowhere,
paralleling the thoughts of what she would eat for dinner, her right arm

began to itch. She touched it softly, just like she might touch Brendan. She ran her finger up her wrist and when she let go, the sensation heightened. It turned electric. Her wrist was itching from the inside and the only way to relieve it would be to cut it open.

She started the car then and drove to Hale's only mental hospital. She told them the same story she'd told what seemed like a hundred times before, and they took her purse, and in return gave her fuzzy socks with little rubber grip things on the bottom.

A man in white appeared in the doorway. He was cute, with no external proof of the scars that life may or may not have left on him. His hair was dark like hers.

Dinner, he said.

Emily and the depressed woman, Sara maybe—she looked like a Sara and Emily hadn't been listening when she'd told her her name—walked down a long hallway to a room with a large oval table. Seven or eight of them were asked if they wanted coffee with their dinner. Emily said that she did, but most of them didn't even answer. Coffee, water, and a plate of food tasting as gray as it looked were set in front of her. As Emily ate, she looked around at the patients sitting at the table. Their eyes couldn't see; she was sure if she waved her hand around, no one would pay her any mind. She was eating at a dinner table full of a family of robots. Emily was looking at empty shells disguised as live bodies; there wasn't anyone in there. No one spoke. There was no music or TV; not a sound embellished the soulless room. They ate, and they left, and one of the nurses yelled something about cigarettes.

Emily lay back down in her bed. She wasn't sure if she would ever do anything else while she was here, but she didn't know what else to do, really. Lie in the hallway? She could dance, but there was no music, and she was pretty sure any sudden movements would earn her a cute white strait jacket.

Another man, not as biologically interesting as the first but with more of a personality, appeared in the doorway. He smiled. You have a visitor, Emily.

Emily got up from the bed and guided her gripped, socked feet against the tile floor until she found Seth in a small visitor's room. He was crying; he had tears on his face. Emily had never seen Seth cry before.

Emily and Seth, Emily's boyfriend, had been together a few years; they lived together. Their relationship was nothing extraordinary except the fact that Seth was a somewhat good boyfriend and treated Emily well. Other than that, well, the sex was bad, he didn't have a job, he was physically unattractive (to her), and Emily was not in love with him anymore. She was bored with him. Maybe that's really why she was here. Maybe she needed some excitement in her life.

Jesus Christ, she thought as she considered the possibility that she had checked herself into a mental institution for some excitement. She really *had* lost her damn mind.

Don't cry, Emily told him as she hugged him. I need you to be strong for me now. Your tears aren't helping.

He sniffled, wiping his face. I'm scared for you, Emily.

Me too.

In that moment an old man with white hair and a white beard walked slowly and calculatedly down the hallway, past the visiting room. He didn't have any pants on.

Seth burst into laughter, and Emily would unfortunately always know what the term *old balls* referred to.

I've got to get out of here.

Emily. Seth grabbed her hand.

Emily shook her hand free and told Seth to be quiet.

Looking back now, Emily could feel the transition from banally normal to sort of intelligent click on in her brain like a switch, and she thought of Brendan. This is how he would like to see her get out of this situation. In fact, if he was here, he'd probably laugh at what was about to come out of her mouth. She stood up straight and approached the nurse's station. She had never stood up straight in her entire life.

Excuse me. She smiled sweetly, knocking on the station window.

A large man with a shaved head emerged, dressed in white. Yes?

I would like my purse, please.

I'm sorry?

My purse. You confiscated it when I arrived here. I would like it before I leave.

You can't leave.

Excuse me? Emily asked incredulously, her eyes bulging out of her head. I'm sorry, am I . . . a prisoner? Have I committed some sort of crime and am being held against my will now?

The nurse stammered. I . . . I . . .

If I walk out that door right now, past that red line, Emily pointed to the two-inch-thick red line painted on the floor six feet from the door, are you going to chase me?

No, but if you don't sign out, with pre-approval from Dr. Talen, then you will be considered AWOL.

Do I look like fucking *Rambo* to you?

The nurse didn't answer.

I haven't seen the doctor yet. Let me speak to him, please.

He's not here yet.

Emily's stare at the nurse was intense, but in reality, she wasn't staring at him but the stupidity his body reeked of.

Call him. Now.

Seth's voice boomed next to her ear. What the hell are you doing?

Be quiet, Seth.

They waited a few minutes, no words passing between them, and the nurse returned with a clipboard and Emily's two-hundred-and-fifty-dollar Guess purse that her father had bought for her, cell phone and book inside. Emily signed the paperwork and thanked him.

The other nurse—the nice one who alerted her of her visitor earlier—asked her to remove her bedding from her bed and bring it to him.

Emily considered telling him to go fuck himself in an effort to make a grand exit—she would never be back—but he was a nice guy, and she was sure that he got verbally, if not physically, abused enough.

Emily played Molly Maid for the Crazy House, ignoring Sara's questions in the process, and she walked out the double glass doors with Seth tight on her heels.

From the hospital parking lot, Emily inhaled a deep breath through her nose, closing her eyes against the stars in the dark sky, and threw her purse in the trunk of her blue Subaru.

Emily? Seth asked from behind her. Are you sure you're alright?

She whirled around, facing him. You have six hours to pack your current life, she said.

What . . . ? The perplexed words written all over his face were readable even under the moonlight. Where are we going?

Emily looked down at the lines painted on the ground. She couldn't even take care of herself, let alone him. But if she told him that he'd try to talk her out of it. And she wanted this to last about 2.5 more seconds. She indulged in another deep breath. Fueled by only pretend confidence, her head snapped up and she looked directly into his familiar dirt-brown eyes.

Pack your shit, Seth, and get the fuck out of my house. Don't ever come back.

CHAPTER THREE

EMILY HADN'T BEEN AT WORK TODAY. She owned this little bookstore downtown called *Danielle's Books*—who the fuck Danielle was, Brendan didn't know—that she had bought with the inheritance her grandparents had left for her. Brendan had gone by to see her, but only her assistant Savannah, a little blonde thing who was very sweet but didn't seem to know much about the world, occupied the space. She'd told Brendan that Emily was sick today.

It was Brendan's experience in his years-long friendship with Emily that she was never far from that which she loved, and there was nothing Emily loved more than books. And that fucking cat. He didn't think she was sick, but it must have been something serious if it had torn her away from her shop. That was part of the reason why he was so surprised to see her tonight. That and the fact that he hadn't seen her for months, probably. It had been a while for sure. When she sort of disappeared a while back, he hadn't expected to see her for quite some time, if ever again. Which is why he went by the shop that morning.

Shore's outdoor patio was set up somewhat circularly. Rustic, beat-up iron tables and chairs atop an old wooden deck were bordered on one side with a somewhat high plank wall. That was its brilliant design. No music played; it was nothing like the inside. It had been designed for a bunch of wannabe hipsters and their cigarettes.

All of Brendan's friends were staring at him from where they sat around the table, but he ignored them. Especially Will.

The thing was, everyone looked at the way Brendan looked at Emily, except Emily. She sat huddled with her back to a corner before the planked wall. She was always setting up reading posts in one corner or another. She was beautiful. Not right now, but she could be. Brendan couldn't see her violet eyes as they stared down at the book in her hands, but her jet black hair glimmered under the dim street lamp, however frizzy it was at present. Dark freckles speckled a bridge over her nose from cheek to cheek. Her lips were thin, like a bird's beak. She hadn't been kissed in a while. Brendan switched his focus to the book in her hands. He wouldn't ever stare at her for too long, for fear of getting sucked into her dark hole.

Memoirs Aren't Fairytales, the book was called.

No, they weren't. Not for her anyway.

Brendan had asked her about her childhood once. She'd told him that her last childhood memory was when she was three years old. She was sitting in the rain with her father in the backyard; Emily loved the rain. Her father wanted her to sit on his lap so they could watch the lightning storm, but Emily refused. She said that she had this reservation about being closer to the sky when the lightning hit, as if she'd be safer on the ground.

Brendan thought it strange that she couldn't remember anything after she was three.

"Oh, I have memories," she had said. "But they're not any good. Childhood—it's not supposed to be like that, you know?"

Brendan didn't know.

He got up from the table where he sat, ignoring Will's eyes as they followed him, and approached Emily. He waited for her to look up. She did, and smiled.

Brendan wanted to slap her. What the fuck was she smiling for? It was the most illegitimate gesture of happiness he had ever seen. He stared at her so hard, his eyes started to hurt.

Emily looked away, at the street, her smile dropping to the ground and disappearing into a dark puddle. It was as if Brendan had in fact slapped it right off her face.

"Get up."

Emily would never let anyone speak to her that way. But Brendan wasn't anyone. Emily belonged to Brendan. In some sort of fucked up way.

She got up.

*   *   *

Emily was four when the universe yanked her childhood from her grasp.

She was in a room in a location she didn't remember. Her mother, Karla, had moved her around too much after she had left Emily's father for her to remember every house they lived in, every school she went to. It was every year, sometimes twice or three times in a year.

Emily was lying in bed. It was dark—her mother didn't believe in night lights for four year olds, apparently. She wasn't scared of the dark at that time, just as she didn't fear it now. Her life had been a sandwich of fear. With all the bad parts trapped on the inside.

She couldn't sleep when she was a child. From those corners of fear, amongst the photos on the walls, the wall paint, the walls themselves, emerged shadows. Dark, strange, mysterious, bizarre, horrific shadows. They clawed at the walls, crawling downward and inching towards the floor. Beneath her bed was a pool of blackness that looked to her like the sticky pools at the La Brea Tar Pits. Except, the carpet in her childhood room was white.

They spoke to her. They still do. It's in a language that doesn't exist, in a tone that no person trying to get the message across would ever use. A dark, deep man's voice whispers the words Emily cannot understand. At four years old, his imaginary lips were right next to her ear, whooshing the words at her like a violent wind, threatening to dry out her skin until it cracked open and let him inside.

Emily couldn't remember what she did at the time; how she reacted. She didn't remember being scared, but she was four. And she used to have these panic attacks in the middle of the night, so . . . who knows.

She had told Seth about them once. She was twenty-three. He was scared. He shook his head and told her to stop talking because she was freaking him out. She told her mom, too, in her early twenties. Karla, Emily's mother, couldn't believe that she didn't notice what her daughter was going through. She kind of laughed, then. It was strange to Emily how a conversation about her hearing voices at four years old turned into a conversation about Karla being a shitty mother and inevitably earned a giggle. Even stranger is the fact that she would think it was strange, since that's the only kind of behavior Emily had ever known from a mother.

Now, the voices just irritated her. Not when she's home, she doesn't care about sleep; she'll sleep when she's dead. But in public, in broad daylight? When she was in college, or at *Danielle's*, at *Shore*? She struggled. To be normal. To appear normal. But she wasn't scared of the voices now.

She connected the comfort her own insanity brought her with the warm sensation she felt in her chest when she looked at Brendan. He didn't scare her. People, in general, scared her, but Brendan Tanner didn't.

He was sort of beautiful.

He was just a regular guy. Not even. He looked like a bum. His dark brown hair was always disheveled. Not in a hipster way, in that he used some product to make it look like that, because he didn't. It just grew that way. He had this beard thing that was uneven most of the time. He had arms but didn't show them. He wore whatever. Jeans and a plain t-shirt. Or shorts when the weather would permit it, which was basically always in Southern California. He'd go around naked if he could; the man hated clothes.

Emily had never seen Brendan naked, but even clothed, he was sort of beautiful. To her.

He enveloped her in his weirdly sexy scent that she could never describe or duplicate when he forced her into a hug that lasted some indeterminable amount of time. She didn't pull away like she did with everyone else. As if it would do any good anyway. She preferred to keep her bones and limbs in working condition, and if she pulled, Brendan would pull harder. Brendan was strong, stronger than Victor, Emily's hulk of a friend whose arms would snap a rubber band if he flexed. Brendan could easily kill any man with his bare hands if he wanted to. He almost did once when some guy punched him in the face for no reason. Luckily for the man, woven through his anger like a string, was Brendan's own reminder in his head not to kill him. The guy got knocked out after a single hit from Brendan, though.

He let go of her when a soundless tear dribbled onto his neck. Emily wiped her bare cheek on his shirt as he pulled away. She sat down and picked her book back up, attempting to read.

The left side of her face was fucking burning.

She looked at him as he sat down next to her.

He stared at her. His face was expressionless; the polar opposite of Seth's from earlier. A bona fide blank page with invisible words on it: unreadable. She didn't know what he was thinking. Feeling. She wasn't him, so how could she know? But Brendan would expect her to know and would probably get mad if she didn't. Like she was a telepath and was failing at her trade.

Are you listening to me?

Brendan's intense gaze broke as he looked across the table. Victor was there, watching Emily. Her friendship with Victor was so weird. They rarely ever spoke or hung out outside of *Shore* when *The Authors,* Brendan's band, played, but she could tell him anything with an unspoken disclaimer of secrecy. He would never repeat anything that shouldn't be repeated. He didn't judge. He was incapable of being swallowed by inconsequential shit. He just existed, being there when she needed him, and in some faraway land when she didn't. He knew about Emily's illness, while Brendan didn't. He was the perfect friend.

I am now, Brendan said. Victor, sir. They shook hands.

Where's Seth? Victor asked her.

I broke up with him. Emily didn't hesitate.

She ignored Brendan as Victor asked her if she was okay.

Fine.

Kat made her way around the table and bombarded Emily with a tottering, overwhelming hug while shouting some bubbly greeting that Emily tuned out. Kat's positive energy was disgustingly refreshing. She was a bubbly cheerleader of life. She lived a problem-free, drama-free life—which a lot of people did—but she took it to the extent that if you had any negative thing you wanted to share, she'd drop your friendship without a moment's notice. One was not allowed to be hurt or unhappy around her. And if you were, she did not care.

Jace—the only male friend in Emily's life who made her feel like one of those witty, down, geek girls, like being a nerd was cool—followed. Their somewhat new friendship was based solely off of comic books and witty banter, but he didn't say anything tonight. He just stared at her like he knew something she didn't. She ignored him.

The friends here tonight knew better than to occupy the seat to her right. Mia practically knocked Emily down with her hug in the very moment she stood up as Mia approached. Theirs was such an unlikely friendship of the masses. On her birthday card last year, Emily had written 'to the highly unlikely friendship I never want to lose.' It was her own mysterious way of connecting with her friend who, like her, had an unlikely pregnancy that never produced a child. When Mia read the card, she had cried.

Emily had an abortion once, when she had first gotten with Seth several years before. Seth had gotten into this thing wherein he wanted to finish inside her when they had sex. She was taking the morning after pill every time this happened. She couldn't take birth control; it made her sick. The first time, the morning pill worked. The second time, not so much. She had known she was pregnant before she took the test; it was inevitable. You didn't get lucky all the time, if ever. They went back and forth between whether to have the baby and not at least five times. When they finally decided to have the child, Emily had written down pregnancy instructions for herself in a journal—food she wasn't supposed to eat, vitamin information, etcetera—she didn't know anything about being pregnant at twenty-two years old—and absently left the journal out. Seth had called her at the bookstore.

I don't want to be a father, he had said. And she didn't argue. She had been born to at least one parent who didn't want her, and she knew exactly how that had turned out.

She'd already had a name picked out for her daughter. Logically, she had no way of knowing the baby would be a girl at that time—she had been six weeks pregnant—but, she just *knew*. As lame as that sounded.

Okay, she said.

Seth had paid four-hundred dollars for the procedure, but not without asking Emily to pay for half. Emily was pretty sure that the largest waiting room she had ever seen was over-capacity. Most women were quiet, some crying, though probably not out of fear like Emily—she'd never had surgery in her life beyond getting her wisdom teeth pulled— but there was this one woman who brought her sister to drive her who had to shush her. The sister was on the phone, laughing hysterically. She had no respect for the dead, apparently. Or, rather, the soon-to-be-dead.

A woman Emily assumed to be a nurse called her name, and she reminded Seth that the procedure would be over two hours later. He had the memory of a goldfish. She was given a hospital gown and shoved into a room with more than ten other women. No one spoke. They took blood one at a time. This one woman had a tubular pregnancy, which is one of the most painful experiences a woman can go through. As they inserted the needle in her arm to take her blood, she doubled over in pain. She rolled out of her chair, and a blood-curdling scream escaped her tiny body as she writhed on the floor. As they rolled her out of the room in a wheelchair, she was still screaming.

Just give me the D&C! she had commanded, which of course they couldn't do. She needed a Laparoscopic surgery, which was a procedure that they didn't perform at the clinic. Emily imagined her screaming in the ambulance the entire way to the nearest hospital.

This young girl—she couldn't have been a day over sixteen—began to cry next to Emily.

I can't do this, the girl cried. I can't deal with this right now.

Emily's instinct was to comfort her, take her outside of the room and hug her like the girl's mother might, but she was not in the frame of mind to even move at that point, let alone speak.

She was taken into another room where a nice female doctor stuck her gloved fingers in Emily's vagina while she took an ultrasound.

How long have you been sexually active? The doctor asked Emily.

Six years.

Have you ever had an abortion before?

No.

You've been careful. Unfortunately, this time, though, not careful enough. Don't ever let me see you back here, all right?

You won't, Emily said, tears streaming down the side of her face as she lay on her back with her legs wide open. I can assure you of that.

She was led into a large room with beds strewn about, most of them occupied. Most of the women appeared to be asleep. She lay down, and they injected her with something. They told her to count backwards from one-hundred.

When she woke up, she remembered getting to ninety-seven but had no idea where she was. She was covered with a sheet, and there was some type of cotton material rubbing against the inside of her thighs. It was makeshift underwear—a thick pad with straps attached that was already around her legs. She eventually figured out she was supposed to pull it up, and she did.

In a stall guarded by a nurse, Emily dressed in her sweats and t-shirt that she had worn in. Returning to the room where screaming-girl had collapsed, she heard a woman—the one who had brought her obnoxious sister—tell another woman that her husband didn't even know she was here. She already had five children and didn't want another one. This was her sixth abortion.

They gave Emily crackers and orange juice in a small carton like the ones they gave you in school.

They pulled her into a small room with a phone and told her discreetly, your driver isn't here.

With the phone, she called Seth's cell phone.

Hello?

Seth.

Baby? He asked her incredulously.

What are you *doing*?

Watching TV? He asked, as if he wasn't sure.

Well. If it's not too much to ask, could you come pick me up please?

Through the phone she could hear the slap of his palm as it connected with his forehead. *Idiot.*

I'll be right there.

She waited about twenty minutes. He arrived, and she was escorted in a wheelchair out the back door. In the nicer clinics like this one, they wheeled you out a back door so you didn't have to do the walk of shame through the lobby. Why they felt the need to wheel her out after she had just walked from the bed to the room to another room, she didn't know.

She got in the car, and Seth started in immediately. Emily, I'm so sorry, I thought I was supposed to get you at three o'clock, are you—

Seth, be quiet and drive me home, please.

He didn't have anything to say to that.

On their way out, Emily caught sight of a woman on the sidewalk holding a sign. It said *I regret my abortion.*

Emily didn't have anything to say to that.

Mia was the only person on this earth who had heard that story. Emily had told her at some gourmet pizza kitchen that served good wine. Mia and Emily had been more alike than anyone would imagine. Externally, Mia was nothing like Emily. She was fashionable and exotic and perfect. The truth was, though, that Emily believed Mia was her soul mate and essentially, a reflection of her. They joked that if their respective relationships with men didn't work out, they'd metaphorically come out of their respective closets and announce to the world that they were in a romantic relationship together.

I'm getting married! Mia squealed.

Mia had been dating a lovely man of God for a couple years, a gentle, model-material of a man who smiled at all the right times. Emily didn't know him as well as say, Brendan, but based on the way Mia's eyes were glistening under the moonlight, Emily knew Mia thought it was the right thing to make her happy.

I'm so happy for you, Mia, Emily said.

She squealed. The wedding is September eighteenth. You have to come.

You know that's my birthday, right?

Mia recovered quickly. She had planned her wedding on her best friend's birthday and hadn't even known the difference. Also like Emily, she was a damn good liar. Well then it will be an extra special day, she said, smiling.

She hugged her. Of course I will be there, Emily promised.

Emily closed her book and left it on the table as the group got ready to go inside for the show. The bookish people in Emily's life would never leave a book somewhere, never lend it to someone without a written contract detailing a promise to return it without harm, but that seemed so dense to Emily. It was as if a doctor told you about this great medicine that would cure your cancer, but kept it in a locked box. There were so many great things in this world, and they should be shared with those less fortunate. Books could heal people too.

CHAPTER FOUR

WHEN EMILY WAS NINE and her brother Derek two, she woke up in the middle of the night to a bang. Her stepfather, Derek's father, was yelling. His name was Seth. When Emily was ten, she promised herself she'd never get in a relationship with anyone named Seth.

She removed the covers from Derek's bed, across the room from hers, and cradled him into her arms. She carried Derek to her bed and covered their heads with her covers. She wrapped her arm around the back of his neck while pulling him close and covered his ear with the palm of her hand.

Emily heard her mother scream. She was stoically still. Tears burned her cheeks, but she didn't dare make a sound.

There was another bang, and the screaming stopped. Emily heard the front door slam, and then: nothing.

She fell asleep, eventually. She never let go of Derek.

Emily asked her stepfather where her mother was when she awoke. Her question bled dominance, even in the voice of a nine-year-old girl. She should have been scared of him, but she wasn't. By that time, she was already waiting to die.

In response to her question, the front door flew open and her mother came marching inside. The left side of her face was black. There was a purple ring around her neck, the color of the hula hoop lying on the grass in the backyard. She was limping on her right leg.

Pack your shit, Karla said to Emily. We're leaving.

Emily, Derek, and their mother, they left. And they never went back. Emily had to hand it to her mother, who was never really a mother at all, for her loyalty. If he had touched Emily or Derek, she would have killed that motherfucker.

Brendan's music didn't remind her of a bang, like a lot of music did. Brendan was truly, and undoubtedly, a rare musician, and it showed.

While the rest of *The Authors'* fans head-banged, or whatever, Emily tended to unknowingly sink into her seat, the inside of her head rattling slightly with each and every one of Brendan's rifts entrapping her. The small space of *Shore's* interior, its occupants' presence, and even the time disappeared. But it wasn't just Brendan that filled this lounge every Friday night, obviously. Every aspect of their music was intoxicating: each instrument blended into the next to collaborate that perfect melody while standing alone discernibly and independently. The voice of William Young was something to be celebrated as intensely as Brendan's musical passion. His voice, dominant against a faint melody, anger accompanying utter musical domination, dissipating during a squealing solo—it was so true, so real, it had the power to force one sensation into despair, rage, love, grief, or tranquility, embedding into you the very sensation the music dictated.

Music has the power to brand its own negative emotions upon your soul. But sometimes, sometimes it's that very melody that fuels the memory that preempts the feeling, and that makes you happy, not sad. That was why Brendan made music. To fuel the memory and the ecstasy you experienced in that single moment, not the pain laced with regret you infinitely felt afterwards. Emily couldn't relate to music that way, but Brendan could. And tonight, like every night, he did.

But then the music stopped and Brendan opened his eyes, and Emily was sad. Emily was sad, until she was scared, when Brendan collapsed on stage.

*   *   *

Brendan felt nothing. He saw nothing.

He knew nothing.

But that didn't matter.

The swollen crowd before the stage was really of no consequence to him. His music consumed him. Destroyed him. Sealed him.

He didn't even really exist.

Until he did.

Brendan breathed sharply, cutting his heart open. The flaps of his heart spread freely like the wings of a butterfly. His fingers lost their grip and his pick bounced off the stage with a crash in his ears. The deep waves from Tom's *Warwick* behind him could not compete with the sound. His knees bent, knocking the wooden planks beneath him. He flattened his palm at the edge of the stage as he gasped for air. He coughed. Will was at his side; Brendan felt his touch, heard his voice, but . . .

Brendan opened his eyes and slowly lifted his head.

She had this walk. She was so reserved about her physical appearance—Brendan didn't think he had ever even seen her feet—but the way she walked, floated, was like she was the sexiest woman in the world, and she knew it. Her hips swayed like a feather in the wind when she walked. Brendan was behind her on the stairs once, at his house. And in that moment, he really didn't want anything more than to stick his dick in her ass.

Emily stood in a far corner—always backed into a corner—a dark, empty crevice of the bar free of people, with an expression that told Brendan—and everyone else—that he was supposed to be intimidated by her.

He wasn't.

"Brendan," Will called beside him, gently shaking him.

"Will," Brendan croaked out in a whisper, "please stop talking."

Brendan untangled himself from his guitar and set it gently upon the stage. It probably should have occurred to him earlier that he had stopped playing in front of a full crowd, but he really didn't care.

Will was glaring at Brendan, but Brendan ignored him.

Brendan stepped over his guitar and leaped from the stage. Strolling through a cluster of tattoos that a twice-stricken criminal wouldn't take credit for, he held Emily's unwavering glare from across the bar. The look in her eyes reminded Brendan of a caged animal.

Brendan didn't stop.

He clutched her tiny hips between his fingers, lifted her from the barstool, and slammed her against the wall.

The universe didn't make a sound.

Brendan was so drunk.

He clutched her face in his hands.

"He's gone. You can be happy now, okay?"

"Brendan—"

"No. I love you, okay? You are so amazing—you don't even know the effect you have on people by just walking into a room, Em. You have every tool at your disposal to dig deep in that huge heart of yours and find happiness. None of the other shit matters. None of it."

Brendan let her go. The look she gave him was one Brendan, in four years of friendship, had never seen on her face. Before that moment, he hadn't ever known what she looked like.

She was so fucking beautiful.

At the end of their set, Brendan joined Will at the bar. Will was at least six feet deeper in an ocean of alcohol than Brendan was, but Brendan was way more intoxicated than Will; his tolerance was nothing compared to the best friend who was drunk more often than he was sober. Carefully setting his guitar on its back atop of a clean space on the wooden platform, Brendan chose a stool next to Will. Laurie, the bartender, nightly with shirts too small to adequately restrain her less-than-natural breasts (or more-than-natural, rather), presented Brendan with a vodka-and-something. He set it aside, leaning over his guitar and resting his cheek on its delicate strings.

In the petite crimson body leading up to a thin 22-fret rosewood board, opposite a glossy mahogany neck, tipped with a matching red headstock which housed its name in elegant gold lettering, the guitar was currently the love of Brendan's life. His Firecracker.

He kind of had a thing for redheads. They were all fucking crazy, though. All anyone had to do to verify that was to ask Will.

"Brendan."

If it had been a woman's voice, Brendan would have believed that his guitar had just spoken to him. The voice, however, he knew like the calluses sheltering his fingertips. He would have ignored him but he never called him Brendan so he was definitely pissed or worried or both.

Brendan rolled his eyes up at him. Will was a good looking guy. Darkness intensified him throughout. A shade of darkness that was his black hair spiked around his head, contrasting his green eyes that were almost always scowling against his chiseled jaw and defined features. He kind of looked like Emily, actually.

Will was an asshole. Not to Brendan, but to most people. He had once told Emily to shut up because 'men were talking.' At the time,

Brendan had been genuinely surprised that Emily didn't punch him in the face right then and there. It hadn't always been that way, though. He hadn't always been that way. Whether or not the world would ever get any genuine piece of William Young back, Brendan didn't know. Probably not.

"What the hell was that?" Will practically whispered.

Brendan ignored him.

"*Bren.*"

That's better. Brendan looked at him underneath lazy eyelids, and Will stared back at him over a clenched jaw. Will would never intentionally pester him. He would never dig sharp claws into Brendan's temples until he succumbed to the equivalent of torture and spilled his thoughts through his vocal chords. Will understood better than anyone that when Brendan wanted to be left alone, attempting to force him to talk was not only unproductive but impossible. He would walk away. That is, in any situation other than this one, apparently. Will's expression screamed at Brendan.

"It just happened, Will. There's nothing I can do about it now."

"What just happened, exactly?"

"I don't know." Brendan closed his eyes and inadvertently sighed. "I won't remember any of it tomorrow anyway."

"What does that have to do with anything?"

Brendan inhaled sharply through his nose, and deep in his chest, he clutched onto his own breath until the blackness overtook him. "Because I'm drunk, and I don't really love her."

It was the truth, and Will knew that. He would have never said what he said if he was sober. Brendan didn't give a fuck about anything or anyone unless he was drunk.

Not even Emily.

CHAPTER FIVE

EMILY LOST HER VIRGINITY in an elevator.

She loved him. He didn't love her, but it was what it was. It hurt, and then it was over.

Emily's relationship with her father was non-existent by that time—she had moved in with him three years before when he asked her to. After not seeing him at all for the previous ten years, their relationship was good. She was always full, he bought her things; she was at the mall like three times a week. But as she got older, Emily realized that her father didn't know how to have a teenage daughter, and she didn't know how to be a teenage daughter. Everything he said irked her, and she was not nice about it. He'd once told her that if she didn't stop being a bitch that he would kick her out of the moving car they were driving in. He wasn't serious, obviously, but when a father says that to a hormonal sixteen-year-old, it is bound to light a fireball of hatred inside her. If she really wanted to be a bitch, she could call social services. Her dad had already pushed her once when she had lied to him about where she was. Thrown a chair when she first got her period and refused to take ibuprofen. Though she didn't know whether or not it was necessarily his fault, and did love him, Emily could definitely say that during her teenage years until she moved out the day she turned eighteen, her father was not a good father. To her. His anger and frustrations with a daughter who thought for herself, even at that age, always came first, and it was always in the way.

At sixteen, Emily was getting drunk, doing drugs, and having sex. Lots of it. She'd slept with more men than she could count on one hand, all older than her. She didn't know if that was a teenager rebellion thing or just an Emily thing.

She couldn't remember how she met this one group she hung out with. They had their own place and her high school friends were always over there getting fucked up.

One night, Emily was there by herself without her friends, more trashed than she could ever remember being. She didn't know where she was, how she got there, none of it. She woke up on a bed. Her pants were off. He was on top of her: some guy. She couldn't even remember his name now.

She told him no. She was on her period. That was her reasoning at the time for not having sex. She tried to push him, but he was too strong. His dick was inside her, pushing her tampon upwards into her body.

Silent tears were rolling down her face.

She passed out—from the alcohol or the pain or the despair, she didn't know.

She got tested after that. Miraculously, she was clean. After her own close encounter, Emily never had sex again, until she met Seth.

As she walked with Brendan to their cars in silence, she thought that maybe she should be irreparably damaged from that experience as a teenager. That she would hate sex, or it would be difficult for her. But it wasn't. The truth was that Emily Colt loved sex as much as any sexaholic going to meetings like they were AA or something. But she, to this day, still had no idea what good sex felt like. She'd heard her girlfriends discussing great sex time and time again, but if she'd had great sex up until that point, then it wasn't as great as anyone made it out to be.

No one said goodbye when the show was over, drinks were taken away and coffee replaced them. Everyone just kind of dispersed, leaving Emily and Brendan.

Will you caravan with me home? Brendan asked her when they arrived in the parking structure.

Emily nodded and followed him. She parked behind his car, but she didn't get out. She opened her door, and positioned herself sideways in the seat so that her feet were flat on the asphalt. She didn't know what he wanted from her, what she was doing here, and didn't know how to act or what to do with herself, physically or emotionally. She'd be safer in the car.

Brendan knelt on the ground between Emily's knees.

In that moment that she gazed down at him, taking in his soft features, Emily truly believed she would never see Brendan again. That their years of a practically silent friendship would be for naught, because he loved her, but the universe wouldn't let her have him. Because the universe didn't grant beautiful things like Brendan Tanner. Not to girls like Emily. Over time, she forgot that she ever had this thought. And once, in the many years that followed, when she remembered, she wished more than anything that she had kept it in mind. That Emily Colt wasn't good enough for Brendan Tanner and never would be.

You're never going to forgive me for this, she said. I'm sorry.

She kissed him. His lips were warm. His mouth on fire.

Emily was on fire.

His hand was on her neck, choking her. She had never been choked in a sexual situation, or in any situation, before. She invited the pain. Any feeling was better than the absence of it, and every day she craved the kind of physical connection laced with the chemistry that currently passed between them. This physical feeling was the best that Emily had ever had.

He rose from the ground and, with his other hand, he squeezed her hip. Emily screamed. He was on top of her; the center console dug into her spine. She unconsciously arched her back, rising to his stiffness. He groaned, tightening his grip and biting her bottom lip hard.

He pulled away and took her by the hands and pulled her out of the car. He wrapped her in his arms. Over his shoulder, the moon was full.

Beautiful night, Emily whispered.

You're beautiful, he replied.

That was the last and only time Brendan ever told Emily she was beautiful.

CHAPTER SIX

EMILY DID SPEED ONCE. Well, more than once. Her friends had done it recreationally. When they found out she'd never done it, they had something of a meth party for her. They all holed up in this house after she got off her restaurant job. She was sixteen.

When it came down to it, Emily didn't want to do it. But they told her it was all for her, and it would be fun. It wasn't necessarily peer pressure; Emily was totally fine with it up to that very moment, until she wasn't. But she did it anyway.

They smoked it.

The smoke reminded Emily of vaping. There is this huge vaping community, wherein mechanical products and accessories are offered to produce the biggest vapor cloud off of an e-cigarette. The thicker, the better.

Smoking speed is like that. Except it doesn't taste like white gummy bear or banana peach smoothie. It tastes like burnt asshole. Not that Emily would know what that tastes like.

Her ex-boyfriend at the time—he had broken up with her a few weeks before for her refusal to have sex with him—didn't want her to do it. He did meth too, but he didn't want Emily doing it. She remembered instant messaging him and him asking her if she was okay. She'd said she was fine.

She was lying.

Emily was sick. She'd told her friends that she felt like she was going to throw up. They said it just felt like that sometimes, and that'd she be fine. But just in case, to throw up in the cup she had in front of her.

She vomited in the cup. She was so proud of herself, having not been messy about it. Not a drop on the carpet.

That cup would be known as Ralph for years after that.

Emily was sick for three days. She never vomited again, but felt nauseous. To this day she was overly cautious and fearful of the stomach flu. Of any flu, really.

She was dating this guy, sometime after. A real piece of work: meth addict, hardcore criminal, years older than Emily had been.

Noah was his name. He was sitting in Karla's living room with her and Emily. He wanted to smoke speed and wanted Emily to do it with him. She refused. This was sometime after he had taken her to some outing in some desert in a car with some friend. He had tried to pressure her so many times into doing it with them that night that his friend told him to leave Emily alone.

Do you smoke weed? His friend had asked Emily.

Yes.

I wish I would have known; I would have brought some for you. I'll bring some next time.

Thank you.

Emily remembered Noah telling her that he just wanted his friends to like her. At the time, Emily didn't know that you had to be a certain way for your friends to like you. She guessed that she still didn't know that, since she didn't know how to be anyone other than Emily.

So Noah was practically begging Emily to smoke meth with him, right in front of her mother and, for what seemed like the hundredth time, she shook her head no, like a child refusing cough syrup. Which she was, basically, a child at seventeen, refusing something that would make her feel better.

Just do it, Emily, Karla had said.

So she did it.

Emily didn't even have enough sense to be upset about it at the time. She was just scared. Scared that there wasn't a soul in this world who had her back. Not even her own mother.

She didn't get sick that time, but she did get addicted to meth and smoked it every day for six months after that. Until she began to watch herself slowly turn into her mother; and quit on her own without anyone's help.

Marijuana was something Emily and Seth did together during their relationship, but she had stopped smoking a few months ago. They were at a concert, getting high in the crowd like anyone would do at a reggae concert. The crowd was dense; she couldn't step any which way without bumping someone. She was hitting the pipes and joints that were being passed to her faster than she could count them. The bass began to rumble in her chest, and she couldn't breathe. She could hear the drums inside her head. She had to get out of the crowd. She took Seth by the hand and basically moshed through three hundred people. They listened to the rest of show—they couldn't see the band from the back—as they lay on the hard concrete of the venue, watching the stars and holding hands. He seemed upset at the time that she had torn him from his friends, but he didn't say anything.

Every time Emily tried to smoke after that, she'd experience the same anxiety bundled with a paranoia that escalated her illness. Eventually, she just stopped. But tonight, or this morning, rather, all she really wanted was to smoke a bowl.

Emily's house was messy; decorated haphazardly with books and random cheap items she had picked up along the way. She should move, start a new life in a new place, but the truth was she loved Hale too much for that.

She ignored the half-emptied walk-in closet as she opened it—it appeared that all Seth took were his clothes—and found what she was looking for: a single black windbreaker hanging in the corner.

Emily would often wear Seth's jackets outside. Women's jackets available in California were not made for comfort or warmth but for fashion. Emily was very cold all the time, especially her hands and feet—she had bad circulation.

One day she had worn this particular jacket to her store, and while hiding her cold hands in the pockets, she felt something that resembled a plastic bag. In her office, she had found that she had been carrying weed on her all day.

In the closet, she checked the pocket and found it was still there. It was less than a gram probably, but she wouldn't need more than that.

Emily never really had a pipe of her own. Seth had a collection of them in all colors and sizes, but there came a time when Emily wanted one, so they went to Venice and she purchased a bubbler. It was a colorful thing: reds and oranges and blues swirling together in a vibrant rainbow. There was a tiny frog on top that stared at you when you hit it. Emily didn't have a thing for frogs or anything, but in her pot-riddled mind, it was cute. She loved that little frog.

She packed a bowl and sat down on her couch. She was surprised that Seth didn't take the couches at least. He'd bought them. He could have taken anything he wanted. Emily hoped he knew that when he left. He must have known though, since the smiling photos of them staring back at her from the walls seemed deliberate somehow.

Emily hit her bubbler and practically died right then and there. She doubled over, coughing what was left of her lungs. She had forgotten how long it had been since she smoked. She didn't officially smoke cigarettes anymore—with the exception of the occasional drunk social cigarette—and it had been years. Unlike everyone else, it would seem, Emily hated the smell and taste of pot. It tasted like burnt cactus.

She paid her aversion to the taste no mind as she sunk into the couch. She felt her exaggerated care for Everything That Sucked in the World float out of the back of her head. Why the fuck did she quit this shit? God, she would totally walk through life high if she didn't love her bookstore so much.

She guessed that was what she had left to live for at this point. She couldn't give a shit about her family, their drama and their lies. She didn't have a boyfriend to take care of anymore. She just had her books.

She took that back as she felt something rub up against her leg. She closed her eyes and smiled lazily. She had her books and her cat.

Come here, baby, she said.

Iver was a little black cat with shocking green eyes that loved her more than anything she'd ever loved. He hopped on her lap and began to purr. She rubbed his fur between his ears. Emily loved Iver because he never made a sound. Unlike her, he never spoke. Like Brendan, she wished she knew the secret to shutting herself up. If she could get away with never speaking again, she would totally do it.

She supposed she should get up and go to bed. It was five a.m., but she didn't care that much. She could sleep on the floor if she wanted. She had the house to herself. Emily let out this strange giggle that she'd never heard come out of her mouth before.

She felt like she was eighteen again, trading her father's guardianship for freedom.

Emily didn't hear the voices in the following hours. She was free. Just for today.

CHAPTER SEVEN

EMILY DIDN'T TEXT BRENDAN when she woke like he had asked her to when she left the night before. As much as she wanted her happily ever after with him, she wasn't an idiot. They were Brendan and Emily, not Romeo and Juliet; that was never going to happen. Brendan came from a loving, wealthy family. He was intelligent and happy and had everything, and Emily didn't. It wasn't Brendan and Emily and never would be. It was Brendan versus Emily. Good versus evil.

Emily called Mia. She was Emily's go-to. Her real friend. There was Ada, whom Emily had known for twenty years. They talked a few times a year since high school, but it didn't appear that she had cared much for Emily, or anything else than herself, really. Not to mention she was crazy. That meant a lot coming from Emily.

Mia had a best friend like that, too.

Mia and Brendan had been better friends than he and Emily were once upon a time, but not so much anymore, having fallen out of friend-love. So she was Emily's now.

Emily called her.

Hey, love.

Emily was shocked. Mia never answered her phone.

Hey.

What's wrong?

Emily's phone was beeping in her ear from an incoming text message. She ignored it. She knew it wasn't him, and she therefore didn't care.

I didn't tell you this yesterday—I didn't want to spoil your news— but I left Seth.

Whaaaaaat?! Despite her inexorable exterior, Mia was like an emotionally unstable fifteen-year-old when it came to drama. She sounded like a chipmunk.

Yeah.

How?

I told him to get the fuck out of my house.

Mia laughed so hard. Emily had to pull the phone away from her ear. Her laugh was as high-pitched as her squeal.

And then she was Mia.

Are you okay? Do you want to come over?

Nah. I don't. Emily let out this laugh that she knew was spurious. I don't fucking care. Honestly.

Yes you do, she called Emily out.

I do, I said. Just not about him.

Emily didn't tell her who she did care about. She didn't tell her the real reason for her call.

Emily could never tell her what happened between them the night before. It would never happen again, so it wouldn't be that hard keeping it under wraps.

That's not to say Mia didn't already know anyway, though.

The text was from Kat.

She wanted to hang out with Emily and Brendan. Kat liked Brendan; he was a very positive person—albeit in a different way—but still, he was like her. And Kat didn't know Brendan well enough to just hang out with him.

Emily gave Kat some bullshit story about being busy at the shop and to give her a few days.

After a week had passed with no communication between Emily and Brendan whatsoever, Kat texted her again.

Let's go to Bray's. See if he wants to go.

The whole thing was just ridiculous. Emily didn't understand why everyone refused to leave her alone.

She paused on his little picture next to his name on her phone before she texted him.

Kat wants to go to Bray's.

His text didn't come back for the longest thirty minutes of Emily's life. Brendan was terrible with time management.

Are you her personal scheduling assistant now?
I don't fucking know.
Are you going to go?
Yeah.
I'll see you guys around 9 then
This should be interesting, Emily thought.

It was fucking interesting all right.

When Emily was eleven, she went to the refrigerator for a drink. There was a large water bottle on the bottom shelf. Removing it, Emily grabbed a glass and set it on the counter while she set to open the water bottle. Her little hand on the cap, she paused. On the bottom of the frosted bottle was a half-inch thick layer of white powder.

Emily called for her mother and asked her about it. Was that supposed to be there? Water didn't look like that, did it?

TIM! Emily's mother screamed for one of Emily's uncles. Both two-strike criminals lived with them.

Emily was eleven and Derek was four. And there was a meth lab in her refrigerator. Next to the leftover macaroni and cheese.

Emily used to ask Seth if he thought someone had poisoned her wine when they'd go outside to smoke. Seth would just laugh.

No, baby. No one poisoned your wine.

Emily had stopped drinking in public altogether around that time. It was just easier that way. She couldn't remember the transition and what had given her the courage and the confidence to drink in restaurants and bars again. It was probably Brendan. People could say what they wanted about Brendan—he was basically Number One Dick on Earth—but he would never, ever let anything happen to Emily. She believed that.

Bray's was a gourmet burger joint in this charming little college town just outside of Hale. It was the only place it was cool to watch hip bands perform at bars with glossy countertops and play Tasind, a widely popular virtual game, sometimes all in the same day. *Bray's* made their own beer. They had the best burgers Emily had tasted in Southern California. The beer was amazing, not that Emily would know. She wasn't experienced in beer matters. Which is probably why she got so fucked up.

She was acting like a drunk whore of the likes that she herself couldn't stand. She was quiet as Brendan and Kat conducted their conversation. Under the table, she had half her leg over Brendan's when she crossed them in the bar stool she was sitting. They were trying to tell Emily how to do her job. How to play the game of being a business owner. In tone, they talked down to her like she wasn't older than both of them (which she was). They talked down to her like everyone did. Like she was an idiot.

Emily was sort of pissed, but too drunk to be pissed enough to say anything.

Eventually they finished their beers and left. Brendan walked the girls to their cars since they were parked in a separate structure than he was.

Are you cool to drive? Kat asked Emily.

Definitely not. I'm just going to chill in the car for a while and I'll head home. My pad isn't far.

No one knew where Emily lived. No one. Ever. The more people who knew where she lived, the better chance of her mom and family finding out the location, and she couldn't have that. They'd be moved in within two hours.

Brendan hesitated, but Emily didn't even really notice. She initiated a hug goodbye and told him to have a good night. He left.

Emily sat in her car, her own drunkenness intensifying under the darkness of the parking structure. She would have tried to sleep, but she was on the line of spilling said drunkenness in the least desirable way. Her car turning into a spinning rollercoaster wouldn't be beneficial in that moment.

Her phone buzzed.

We could have had coffee or something

Brendan.

Uh. If you want to have coffee . . . or something . . . you have to say so. Not my responsibility.

Uncharacteristically, his reply came immediately.

I'm not looking for a relationship right now, Emily. If that's what you want I can't give it to you. But . . . we could have some fun.

Emily never understood that back then. What men really meant by 'not looking for a relationship.' But Emily wasn't about to ask. She was drunk and she hadn't had sex in like a year.

Emily gave Brendan her address, forgetting all about how drunk she was, and started the car.

CHAPTER EIGHT

SHE WAS NERVOUS.

Her house was dirty, and she had the same clothes on that she wore to work that day, and she was drunk, and her makeup was flaky and runny. She knew she looked like shit without having to look in the mirror, but when Brendan knocked on her door, there was nothing she could do about any of it.

She asked him if he wanted something as she closed the door behind him and walked into the kitchen. Wine, water.

He quietly declined.

She looked at him as she hefted herself onto her kitchen counter. In her house, he looked as awkward as she felt. To her surprise, though, he stepped forward and kissed her. It wasn't like it had been in her car a week before. It *was* awkward, and it wasn't sexy, at all. It felt like two sixteen-year-old virgins who didn't know what the fuck they were doing.

He dragged her to the couch, and they finally began to dance into the rhythm of one another. His hands were on her hips, his fingernails digging into her skin. She grinded her body against his stiffness, her arousal just passing the line of no return. How her pants came off without her having to get up, she didn't know—they were tight and Brendan was under her—but they did, and so did everything else. She should have expected it—this was only going one direction—but when Brendan's dick filled her in one swift motion, she was so surprised that she gasped, and then she moaned.

He lifted her by the hips just slightly, so he could control their movements despite the fact that she was on top, and the lyrics of their bodies flowed in every other way but awkwardly. The sensation was euphoric, and not short, but orgasms had never been easy for Emily—she remembered having one in her lifetime, about two years before—and in that moment she wondered if she should have explained that to Brendan. They'd be going at it for days if his intention was to wait for her to finish first.

Without warning, it seemed, Brendan lifted her high above him, removing his dick from inside her, thrusting her against the wall as he got up. Her cheek was pressed up against it, and it was cool. Her feet were flat on the couch so she was standing on it, her arms practically clawing at the walls. From somewhere behind her, Brendan imprudently entered her yet again, and she began to moan loudly each time she felt him fill her as deeply as he possibly could. One of his hands was pinching her left nipple, and the other hand was on her hip, squeezing hard. Before she knew what was happening, her legs began to shake, and she exploded all over her plush couch. She screamed, but Brendan didn't stop. Even after all the nights Brendan and Emily would be together, it would be the longest and most intense orgasm of her life. He was fucking her and the scent of him was everywhere, and she couldn't stop.

You're still going, Brendan whispered in her ear, laughing slightly, and she screamed louder. He took hold of her clit then, pinching her, and the wind was knocked out of her. She couldn't breathe, and she didn't want to.

I think you need to clean your couch, or something, Brendan said when it was finally over.

They chilled for a while, Emily in sweats and Brendan butt-ass naked on her couch. She thought it strange for a moment, that he'd be so comfortable just chillin' naked in a house where he'd never been before, but Emily realized shortly that it was Brendan they were talking about, and Brendan would be comfortable naked anywhere. Their conversation inside, as inconsequential as it was, didn't last long, though, because Emily really wanted a cigarette, and Brendan's were in his car. So they walked to his car, and they smoked a cigarette, and Emily asked if she could lean on his car or if he would flip out, and he said it was fine because she wasn't wearing jeans and it was buttons on jeans that scratched the paint, which is why most guys flip out when chicks do that. So she leaned on his car, and he asked her why she never wanted to be a mother, which she didn't.

Because my mother Sucks at Being a Mother, Emily answered, and therefore I would Suck at Being a Mother.

Brendan didn't say anything really about her mother, specifically. But he did say that we all fear being too much like our parents and that the only way to get over that was to get over the fear of it.

Emily felt an urge to tell him about her abortion then, but she didn't.

He left—something about a trip with his family early the next day— and Emily lay in bed after receiving a text from Brendan saying that he had made it home okay and asking her to delete their text history. That was when she realized that she had failed to take the photos down of Seth and her. They were still plastered all over the walls. She wasn't holding on to anything—she had fallen out of love with Seth a long time ago—it honestly had just slipped her mind. She was sure that Brendan had felt oh so comfortable as he fucked her on her couch across the wall with the photo of Seth and his sisters.

Emily did remember discussing with Seth the possibility of them breaking up once before, six months before they did. Things in their relationship had already been miserable for about a year; she had been lying in bed—watching TV, not reading, and she hated TV—every moment that she didn't have to be at the shop. She couldn't remember the last time she went out before The Thing Happened with Brendan.

Emily had told Seth she was unhappy, and he basically told her that if she wanted to leave she should leave. Technically, it was their house, but he didn't pay any bills.

I think I'm losing my mind, Emily had told him. Maybe I should see someone.

You should if you think so.

Yeah, I'm going to.

You'll probably have to stop taking the muscle relaxers.

Muscle relaxers. Like her recreational drug of choice had anything to do with the fact that she thought she was literally losing her mind, or the fact that she wanted to do something about it.

Like Emily would choose drugs over life.

Emily wasn't her fucking mother.

That night with Brendan was the last day she took her anti-psychotic and anti-depressant medication. Ever. Meth labs, abusive fathers, and rape had nothing on what she would go through in the months after that; it was the most difficult time in her life. All she had that was good was her nights with Brendan. All she had was sex.

Was it just sex, though, or was it love? Towards the end of the not-relationship that spanned for years and years after that, she wouldn't even be able to tell the difference anymore.

Brendan had stopped responding to Emily's casual texts.

Still, Emily didn't think she would ever see Brendan again, but she refused to let go of their friendship, even if they were to transform into phone friends: a long-distance relationship between two people who were, physically, less than five miles apart. If that's how it had to be—the sacrifice Emily had to make—then, fine. Regardless of how many times Brendan ignored her, she'd never stop reaching out. Emily and Brendan were, first and foremost, friends. They always had been. They laughed together; they threw things at each other like drink straws and loose change. They shared a mutual love for things like chocolate-covered expresso beans and people who were genuine. He comforted her when irrational fears like going to the dentist set in. He would text her photos of his outdoor adventures.

This . . . *thing* . . . they had, it was out of her hands now and always would be. It was Emily and Brendan or nothing. Emily believed that down to the core of her black soul, and she couldn't give them up.

Emily had met Brendan at *Danielle's*. He looked lost in the stacks of the YA section of her bookstore, his puzzled expression signaling the obvious fact that he hadn't stepped foot in a bookstore since 1993. He was looking for a birthday gift for his girlfriend at the time, and Emily had made sure that he went home with one of her favorites. Samantha had been like Emily in that way; a sad little introvert who liked books more than she liked people. Like he had given up on so many souls, he gave up on her. Why he didn't give up on Emily in the same way, though, was a mystery to her.

Emily kept running into Brendan after that, at random coffee shops and delis, gas stations, a health food store, and finally, at *Shore*.

They developed a friendship that was as easy as breathing. But that was over, it would seem. She hadn't spoken to him in weeks. She'd stopped going out again; she wasn't about to force her presence on him at *Shore* or anywhere else. She could listen to their music and watch videos of them play online as easy as she could go see them in person.

Her shock stabbed her in the chest with a soldering knife when her phone dinged from next to her sometime after one o'clock in the morning. She set her book down—some brilliantly ambitious story about a kid named Billy—and she picked up her phone. She wasn't in denial about who it could be; no one else would text her at this hour. Brendan and Emily were creatures of the night, and she was the only one who wasn't out that was still up. Brendan knew that.

Hey.

Hello, Emily responded.

How are you?

Good and yourself

Wonderful!

He was drunk, obviously, but Brendan was always drunk, so it didn't really make a difference.

What are you doing?

Emily thought about lying, thought about telling him she was out drinking with friends or something, but she didn't see the value in it. She really didn't care if Brendan thought she was a loser because she was, in fact, a loser.

Reading.

Fucking romance novels!

In her house alone with her cat, Emily tilted her head back as she laughed hysterically. Brendan had once accused her of fan-girling on those raunchy romance novels with some striking shirtless man on the cover. At the time, Emily had been appalled.

I don't read that shit, and you know it, you fucking idiot.

He had laughed so hard.

Fuck off, Emily texted back.

Hahaha! I am in no condition to drive at the moment, but do you want to hang out?

Sure. Are you at Shore?

Down the street, yeah. Come. I'll buy you coffee.

After putting some makeup on and trading her sweats for her favorite white sundress, Emily went. It would be the start of a months-long routine that was anything but routine.

* * *

By way of drunk texts, Brendan directed Emily to a bright, wide open alley in Tenside, the little party town where *Shore* was. She heard his boisterous laugh before she saw him. She followed the familiar sound and found Brendan and all his best friends, whom she didn't know but only saw around. Except Will, of course.

She was really surprised. She'd never expected Brendan to invite her anywhere where his friends would be. It was more than likely that he was drunk and wanted sex and wanted it bad enough to invite her out here so she could take him home with her, but still. He could have met her down the street somewhere if that was the case.

Conversation silenced as she approached. She shivered as the night air brushed its frozen fingertips up her bare arms.

Are you cold? An older man to Brendan's left—not old, but older than Brendan and Emily for sure—asked her as he moved to remove his jacket.

No, she waved her hand in front of her, warding him off, I'm—I'm fine, she stuttered awkwardly. Thank you, though.

She's always cold, Brendan said absently.

She ignored him.

I'm Frank. The older man held out his hand. It's so nice to meet you, Emily. He was smiling this genuine smile that Emily didn't understand. Why was he being so nice to her? She was nobody to these people.

You too, Emily said, shaking his hand.

Nice color, Will said, looking down at her pedicured toes. I like blue.

Emily looked down at her feet. It is turquoise, she said, and thank you.

That is *blue*, Will argued adamantly.

It is turquoise, Emily said, and you are fucking color blind.

Next to Will, Brendan practically spit out his coffee as he tilted his head back and laughed turbulently.

Will glared at her. Unlucky for him, Emily was the only person in the world—aside from Brendan—who wasn't afraid of Will. Emily ignored him, sitting down on the asphalt of the alley and removing her sandals.

Brendan looked at her strangely, before walking away from them to speak to another friend of his.

My feet hurt, she said, answering the question that he didn't physically ask.

Why do your feet hurt? the man named Frank asked her.

Because she's wearing fucking flip flops? Will said.

Shut the fuck up, Will. Emily looked up at Frank. They always hurt. I don't know why.

Frank looked over at Brendan where he stood ten feet away and Brendan discretely shook his head. Frank seemed to back up a step then, putting some space between himself and Emily.

She rolled her eyes and ignored all of them.

Tom, *The Authors'* bass player, and two other guys she had never seen before, started talking about religion in a way that was more intelligent than any conversation that was ever brought up on the matter—or any matter—that Emily had heard, and she tried to keep up for a while, but eventually gave up when words that she had never heard or read before began to fall from their lips. The first one was acumen, and Emily stopped listening.

She watched a homeless man dragging an American flag on the ground walk through the alley. When he caught sight of her staring, he stopped to look at her. His eyes cried red tears that bled down his bruised cheeks. His jean jacket had some kind of worn patch on the back that was torn and frayed.

Emily, she heard her name being called fiercely, and her entire body twitched. She looked over at the voice. Brendan was back, looking down at her from above. I said, are you ready?

Quickly her eyes scanned the alley for the homeless man. He was gone.

Yeah, she said, looking back to Bren. Yeah, whenever you are.

He held out his warm hand to help her up, and she took it. He gave her coffee and he gave all his friends hugs goodbye.

Emily tried to ignore Frank as they walked away, but she felt his eyes on her as fiercely as she felt the absence of her mother her entire life.

Emily! a voice called after them as they arrived to her car. Emily turned around. Will was running at her and pulled her far enough from Brendan that he wouldn't hear what he had to say.

You take care of him, Will said.

I will. Emily smiled.

His slits for eyes were not a threat, but a promise. If anything happens to him, Will said, ever, while he's with you, I'll fucking kill you.

I know, Emily said.

Will looked at her then, in a way that she didn't understand. His teal eyes were intense under the dim light of the street lamp. They stared at one another for a long time. His body shifted—to hug her? To touch her? She didn't know, but then he quickly strode away from her, and she didn't call him back.

CHAPTER NINE

BRENDAN HAD HIS HAND between Emily's legs as she drove them back to her place in Hale. She nearly crashed twenty-six times on the four mile drive. He wouldn't let the passion come at her hard enough to allow her to climax; it was just enough to tease her.

Over the course of the following months, Emily would learn that Brendan loved to sexually tease.

Laughing about something or other as they approached her front door, Emily fidgeted with her house keys as Brendan held her arousal in a tight grasp from behind her. She closed her eyes as his surreal scent gained on her. Her head unconsciously tilted backwards. It was starting to annoy her; she couldn't pinpoint it.

His fingernails painted lines of red up the sides of her legs as he deliberately lifted the bottom of her dress and gripped her hips. Her neck was hot beneath the warmth of his tongue.

Are you going to open the door? he whispered in her ear.

Um . . . she whimpered.

She miraculously got the door open.

Their clothes and shoes branded a trail from the living room down the hallway to Emily's bedroom. She had finally managed to take the photos of her and Seth down, and felt, in the moments she was wrapped into Bren like a shiny gift, that she had nothing to hide. It was an odd concept to her, but that's not to say she didn't like it.

If someone were to follow their breaths and look in from the outside world, they would find Emily on top of Brendan in a halfway upright position, one of his hands gripping her hip and the other around her neck. When he let go of her hip and steadily ran his fingertip up the arch of her foot, her body convulsed as the most intense orgasm conquered her. She collapsed onto him with a smack, and he supersonically flipped her over and gave her three more. He disappeared into the bathroom for some indeterminable amount of time—it could have been three seconds or three hours—and through the cell her orgasmic prison kept her senses in, she didn't see or hear him return. She would have fallen asleep like that, never knowing or caring if Brendan had or would ever return to her, but then his warm arms wrapped around her, and she was gently pulled from her reverie. She didn't open her eyes. After her initial bewilderment wore off, a serene swell of air escaped her, and her existence evanesced into him.

And she slept. She slept in Brendan's arms for thirteen hours.

*   *   *

His hand was in her hair, massaging her head, his arm holding her tight against him, as she slept with her breaths in the crook of his neck. He hadn't been intentionally trying to wake her so he could go home. He was without his car after all, but he could have called one of his friends hours ago if that's what he really wanted. He hadn't been trying to wake her for any specific reason—he felt sort of guilty; he'd never seen any person sleep so peacefully except maybe himself—but the truth was that Emily loved to be touched. She went around acting like that was not the case, refusing hugs from people and ruling personal space, but she loved it. It's why their sex was so good, he decided. It was his hard touch and his ubiquitous presence that made her come so fervently, and the very reality that the electric sensation of his hands set her off (more than once in a night) is what set him off. He guessed maybe that indirectly made him a narcissist, but he didn't fucking care.

Brendan had fucked a lot of women over the course of his manhood. He'd be lying to himself and everyone else if he said that women didn't flock to him, though he didn't know why. But never like this. If his humanly flawed body would allow it, he would fuck the shit out of Emily for days. It wasn't her body or her aesthetically pleasing face or her dripping vagina, necessarily, but the reaction she gave. It was her reaction to him that was the reason he was here right now. She was so sexy, and he couldn't get enough of it or her. He didn't know if it—this—would ever be enough.

When Brendan looked back at the moment that he was watching Emily sleep as if he were some creepy dude from a book that Emily may or may not have liked to read, he would have liked to say that she woke gently, blinking her eyes open and smiling under the afternoon light that snuck through the blinds, but that's just not what happened. She woke with a start, her body convulsing in his arms. He held her tightly as she gasped, forcing air into her constricted lungs. The beat of her heart against his chest reminded him of his drummer Weston's double bass. The right thing to do was to ask her if she was okay, but clearly that would be a stupid question.

"Sorry," she whispered, swiping her hand across her face to remove the hair from her eyes.

He tucked her face back into the crook of his neck, massaging her head with his fingertips again, and asked her if she had heard the latest from *The Cotes*. She hadn't.

He played it on his phone. Her plump lips formed a smile against his neck, and moisture fell on his chest.

If he had it his way, this would be the only time Emily would cry. Emily would only cry tears of joy when art took hold of her heart. Brendan's definition of art was that which made you feel something. And there was no art like Emily Colt. In order for her to achieve such happiness, all he had to do was make her fall in love with herself.

Of course, only she could do that.

*　　　*　　　*

It was pretty easy to forget about Brendan when there were others around that forced their presence upon Emily. She'd really only spoken to Ada, her best friend from junior high, all of five times in the past three years. But Ada had somehow gotten wind that something was up and had texted Emily out of nowhere.

Everything okay?

Yeah, I'm good. But Seth and I broke up.

Oh no! Are you sure you're okay?

I'm fine.

In that case . . . let's go get trashed. We'll have a breakup party!

Ada was fucking nuts, obviously. But Emily was . . . well.

I'll see you on Friday.

Ada wanted Emily to join her and her boyfriend Mark, whom Emily had never met, for dinner, but Emily had stayed at the shop late.

Where are you? her phone vibrated against the wooden surface of her desk in her office.

Yeah, running a bit late. I'll meet you at the bar.

Dammit! I have like five guys here who want to meet you.

Emily's heart flared inside her chest and she let her head fall back against her chair.

Ada, I swear to god I'm not coming if that's how this is going to go.

I'm sorry! It just kind of happened. Come to the bar. It will be just us, I promise.

Gina's was a run-down sports bar with bricks for walls in a corner of their world that no one would ever go to on purpose. But they had cheap drinks, and Ada apparently knew everyone there including the bartenders, so they were basically free. Emily's tab after four hours of drinking would end up costing her a whopping eight dollars.

Ada was a pretty girl, with platinum blonde hair and pink tattoos. As much as Emily would sustain her policy that all humans were insufferable, she had to admit internally that she had missed Ada and it was damn good to see her. They talked like drunk girls would, about failed relationships and about rebuilding a lost friendship. Ada's boyfriend got mad at her when she started to get too drunk, and Emily rolled her eyes, signifying her time to go, until Ada waved Mark off and introduced Emily to a somewhat-cute blonde guy named Terrence. He liked comics and good music and *Disney* movies. He and Emily fell into easy conversation as drunk people so often do, until the bar was closing and they exchanged numbers. He said something like I hope to see you again when he hugged her goodbye.

She arrived home to the ding of her phone when a text came in from Terrence.

I hope you made it home okay.

Emily smiled at her phone, mostly because Brendan never gave a shit if she made it home okay, and she replied that she had.

When she fell asleep somewhat drunk and as content as Emily Colt ever got, she didn't even consider the fact that Bren hadn't responded to her text from five hours earlier. That he was probably out fucking some other girl, and that's why he hadn't replied.

CHAPTER TEN

A WEEK LATER, five weeks since she had seen or heard from Brendan, Emily had plans to go out with Ada again. Ada wanted to get dressed up and go to Hollywood or something or other. Beforehand, Emily had plans to hang out with Terrence.

Arriving at the same bar in a dress that was much too elegant for the entire town, she chatted up a few people she knew from high school while she waited for him. He texted a few times, apologizing for his tardiness due to the washer that took forever to complete its cycle. Due to her father, she wasn't into late people, but it meant something that he wanted to arrive in clean clothes, she guessed. He was a guy, after all.

He looked sort of adorable in a green shirt that matched his eyes. He bought her a drink, and they talked for hours about inconsequential things. It was easy compared to her conversations with Brendan, which tended to bleed with big words while he schooled her on things like how fireworks worked. Terrence told her he was a film snob yet hadn't seen her favorite Peter Sellers movie, and she told him to watch it. Ada arrived after a few hours in tight jeans and knee high boots, and Emily declined her invitation to Hollywood.

The night was pretty uneventful, save for the slight gang activity in the back of the bar and Terrence's drug breaks. He was apparently a dedicated pothead and fucked around with cocaine. Emily gently pushed this to the back of her mind along with the fact that he had an illegitimate child who was basically a newborn (not to mention he didn't have a job). After bar hours, a few of them caravanned to Ada's house, which was right down the street, and drank some more. It couldn't really be called a house as much as a lightless, empty shell, since Ada hadn't yet technically moved in and there were no lamps or furniture except for a single couch in the living room. Emily and Terrence sat on it as Emily waited to hear from Ada. She wasn't back from Hollywood yet, and Emily knew she was really drunk. Emily drove drunk all the time, but Ada wasn't Emily, and that was different, somehow. She laid her head back on the couch and let out a long breath.

I'm sure she's fine, Terrence said gently, and Emily tilted her head sideways to look at him then. He kissed her, and then he said, I've been waiting to do that since last week.

It was sort of sweet if not boring, absent of the dominant passion a kiss with Brendan would entail, but she didn't think about it at the time. He was holding her hand, and she felt like a stupid teenager but didn't really care about that or anything else in that moment.

Emily's phone dinged from the floor where it was charging, and she jumped up in an effort to find out where Ada was and if she was okay. Ada stumbled into the front door, and Emily did a double take between her best friend and her phone.

You think I forgot, don't you? the text read when she finally got around to reading it. It was three a.m.

Forgot what, exactly? Emily replied.

How amazing our sex is.

How could I possibly forget that? Emily played along with his game.

What are you doing?

Chillin' with friends.

Meet me at your house, her phone said.

All right.

Outside, she turned to Terrence smoking a cigarette.

I'm pretty tired, she said. I've got a long drive home. *Lie, lie, lie.* It didn't matter; Emily was good at it. Her mother had taught her well. I'm gonna head home.

Okay, he smiled. I'll walk you out.

Emily said goodbye to Ada and her friends and regretfully kissed Terrence goodbye at the car. He said something, but she didn't know what it was; she wasn't listening.

She eventually found Brendan at her doorstep, and she sighed. That night, her regret trapped her screams and her orgasms inside her. She was such a fucking whore.

Hopefully Brendan was too drunk to notice. Knowing him, that was probably a fair assessment.

*   *   *

Weeks passed again with no communication with Brendan. Terrence wanted to take Emily to a theme park in some effort to be romantic, she guessed, so they double-dated with Ada and Mark. Terrence nearly didn't get in the park because he had missed a payment on his annual pass, which was an embarrassing event for everyone, but he did finagle his way in somehow, and they smoked cigarettes in a shaded designated area. Throughout the day he munched on pot brownies that he had brought with him, and he kissed her on the last dark drop on a water ride, not before telling her he planned to kiss her in that precise spot. He tasted like grass that was on fire and dipped in cheap chocolate. He and Mark disappeared for a while—no doubt for a pick-me-up—before they had a drink at a local bar. Emily found herself buying him things— drinks, whatever—and after a day of him, she couldn't get away fast enough. He was like Seth in most ways, and in the ways that he wasn't, he was like her mother.

She sent him a text when she got home, some bullshit about him needing time to sort his life. She told him to hit her up when he had everything figured out. He never did though, because shortly after, he found a girl who not only would fall in love with him but would do his drugs with him. She was toxic and jealous and ugly inside. Admittedly though, Emily couldn't care less about him or her.

Though she'd never admit it, she was still at a point in her life that she was holding onto something—anything—with Brendan. Even though she knew first and foremost that there would never be any Emily and Brendan; she knew it from the very moment she kissed him in the darkness in her car. It was interesting, she thought, how her own mind had the capacity to trick her into believing something, from the beginning, she never knew to be true.

Over lunch at their favorite organic sandwich shop, Emily told Kat about Terrence. As soon as she told her about his drug use and his fatherhood—or lack thereof—Kat agreed that she had made the right choice. Kat's no-drama policy extended to drug use, and she didn't associate with anyone whose life was ruled by substance.

Which was an interesting thought in itself.

*   *   *

Emily had started smoking cigarettes again. Not in a habitual way like she had before—she never smoked at *Danielle's* for fear of smelling like smoke in front of her customers—but in the evenings, and maybe on the days she took off if she ever took any days off. It was so easy, from her couple weeks with Terrence, and her nights with Brendan, and the remaining time that she was sitting on her balcony by herself reading books. She would be the first person to attest to her addictive personality, and in that regard, she should stop before it escalated into a twenty-four-hour addiction (again), but she just didn't care.

The sound of her phone shocked her out of the dark world that was currently playing in front of her eyes from the book in her lap. She wondered sometimes why she bothered with books. If she wanted to hallucinate, all she had to do was get up in the morning.

She sighed at the screenshot of some sarcastically damaging tweet about *Twilight* that was supposed to be funny.

#mindblown she texted him back, rolling her eyes.

She was very good at the game, but that didn't mean she had to enjoy playing it.

Hahahaha! What are you doing for your birthday?

Going to a wedding.

Ew. Come for drinks after? I'll help you forget alllll about it ;)

Sure.

He was drunk. Guaranteed, he was drunk. Emily would wish on the night of her birthday, that by that time, she had figured out not to take Brendan seriously when he was drunk. Or ever.

Unfortunately, she hadn't.

*   *   *

On the day of the wedding, Emily arrived in her office after a day in the shop to find a voicemail that consisted of Mia singing *Happy*

Birthday very obnoxiously and unorderly. Though any girl would dream to have a girlfriend half as lovely to do such a thing on her wedding day, Emily didn't laugh. She smiled, but when Mia started alternating between the Spanish and English versions of the song, she didn't laugh like basically the entire rest of the world would.

Emily called her back. Are you freaking out yet? she asked Mia when she answered.

Yes! I don't . . . I can't even explain how I'm feeling right now.

Are you sure you want to go through with it?

I . . . I'm past thirty. I can't *not* do it.

So you're going to get married because the rest of everyone you know is married? That's your basis?

It's already planned . . .

And? So people's dinner plans get canceled and you have to alter your dress into a bikini. Your mom's a fucking seamstress. I don't see the problem here.

She giggled, and she told Emily she loved her. I'll see you at seven, she said, and hung up.

Before Emily could stare at her phone in some sentimental or nostalgic way, like some normal girl in some movie about best girlfriends might, the phone rang.

Oh, fuck my fucking life, Emily said to herself, plopping herself in a cushioned chair in the corner of her office and hiding her face between her knees.

She hadn't seen or heard from her in six months or more.

Emily answered the phone. Hi, Mom.

Happy Birthday, honey! Her mom's surreally fake tone infected her ear. She didn't even know how she could discern whether or not it was fake anymore; her mother had never spoken to her in any other voice than she was using right now. But somehow, she just knew.

Hey Mom, Emily said evenly, while digging her fingernails into the back of her leg hard enough to break the skin, if her jeans hadn't saved her.

How are you? I miss you so much. I've been great; I bought a house, and I'm dating a great guy, and I'm thinking about buying a horse . . .

Lie, lie, *lie*, Emily thought as she ceased listening.

. . . So I thought we could have lunch, you, Seth, and I?

Um. Emily cleared her throat. We can have lunch, but Seth won't be there.

WHAT?! Karla all but screamed. Emily Deena Colt! What happened?

I left him.

Why?

Because I was unhappy . . . .?

Oh my god, Emily. I honestly thought you and Seth would be together forever.

Yeah, well.

Come to Michael's for some wine.

I thought you said you were dating a new guy?

I—I—Karla stuttered. I am. Michael and I are just friends, you know that.

Emily's mother had dated Michael for twelve years. The three of them used to smoke meth together in the good old days. The good old days of course being when Emily was a teenager.

Uh-huh. Emily didn't hesitate. If she did, she would never go through with it. I'll be there in an hour.

CHAPTER ELEVEN

MICHAEL'S CURRENT ABODE was in a shittier part of town than *Gina's*, which was to say that he practically lived in what was the equivalent of a run-down Compton. Which wasn't necessarily perturbing to Emily—twenty-five years of experience had taught her to survive—but that didn't mean her gorgeous blue Subaru encompassed the same survival skills. She was going to need to make this quicker than she thought.

Michael and Karla had gone through their share of rented houses over the years just like they had during Emily and Derek's childhood. Michael had been as much of a father as their own respective fathers had been. Back then, when the children called him Mikey, he was as good a father figure as any. That was before he got addicted to meth.

Karla was poisonous in that way. Looking back, every man she had gone through was addicted to some damaging substance when she left him. Including Emily's father.

White paint cracked and chipped off the surface of the structure onto the grassless yard, revealing the old wood underneath. Anywhere from four to six—it was hard to tell—scrapped old cars splayed their bodies and parts haphazardly across the driveway. The iron gate that was missing posts every foot or so was the only symmetrically organized element of the property.

Before Emily could cross the street from where she parked her car, her mother all but skipped out the front door and down the porch steps to wave. Emily! she called. You look lovely! Come in, come in!

Emily followed orders and eventually hugged a wrinkled bag of bones dipped in cigarette smoke. Karla held Emily by the shoulders to get a good look at her. As she complimented her daughter on her beauty, Emily became lost in the face that just a few years before had been a mirror of her own. Under the sunlight of this day, the corners of Karla's eyes drooped down into her cheekbones. There were more lines on her face than a sheet of graph paper. Gaps in her teeth shouted at Emily through the small sound of whispers that Karla's voice actually made. Like Emily, in her prime, Karla was the most beautiful woman anyone had ever seen outside of a magazine or off a red carpet. But in the last six months, Karla had aged ten years. Externally, she was older than Emily's eighty-five-year-old grandmother had been when she passed. In two months, Karla would be fifty-one.

Michael rolled out of his chair as quickly as one of his large size could, rushing over to envelop Emily's small frame in his arms. He was a sweet man with a gray beard. Emily reveled on the similarities of Michael North and Santa Claus; that is, if Santa Claus was a drug addict without any sort of real job.

They sat at a small table in the kitchen that was nicer than anything one would assume to be in this house—refinishing old antiques was a hobby of Karla's—and Emily pulled tissue paper from a gift bag. Like all her other gifts from her mother over the course of her life, she found random items that were probably picked up from somewhere in the house or the cars: body lotion that her mother hadn't liked and some old pajamas that had probably been lying around for thirty years. Emily would throw the bag and its contents away the minute she got home, but even though she secretly loved gifts, she wasn't necessarily bothered by it; Karla had brought Emily up on the premise that it really is the thought that counts, and for the most part, that was true. Even if Karla had spent the birthday money she had saved for Emily on drugs.

Long after Emily stopped listening to her mother talk about Seth and how much of a wonderful man he was, Michael began to laugh.

Karla, he said gently, they're broken up. Why are we talking about this?

Oh, I know, but, oh, do you remember that time you two had that New Year's party . . . .?

As Karla began to laugh, Emily forced a smile that was identical to her mother's own misrepresentation of authenticity. It was easy. Being a liar as good as Emily was a trait that was inherited, not taught.

I have to go, she eventually said.

Oh, I'm sure you have big plans with your friends for your birthday!

I'm going to a wedding, actually.

Who's getting married?

No one you know.

I remember my wedding dress when I married your father, it was so beautiful—

Mom.

Yes, I know, you have to go. Karla got up and kissed Emily's cheek, leaving the soul of her bright pink lipstick on her cheek.

Let's have dinner next week!

Okay, Emily agreed, knowing good and well that was never going to happen. She walked back to her car thinking, even as painful as that had been, it was worth it because she wouldn't have to do it again for a while. She changed her mind about that, though, during her drive home wherein she cried uncontrollably for twenty minutes straight.

*   *   *

Mia's wedding wasn't really a wedding. She wore a white dress and had dinner and cake, but there was no real ceremony that anyone was invited to outside of the most immediate family. They went to a courthouse or something—Emily didn't know—and wanted family and a very limited number of friends (the limited number of friends being one, in this case) to join them for dinner.

At her house, Emily had on a red dress, a gorgeous see-through thing that her grandmother had bought for her before she passed. Her grandmother had been impeccable, even at eighty. Emily was only wearing it because Mia wanted her to, but when she got in her car, she looked down at the bottom of the dress that was basically bunched up at her waistline, and rushed back inside to change. There was no way she could go fraternize with Mia's family in a piece of fabric fit for a prostitute.

She wore the dress she wore to her grandfather's last birthday party, the one her aunt told her made her look like Taylor Swift when she gave it to her while standing in an elegant bathroom in her grandmother's house. The memory of that particular conversation caused Emily to resist the urge to change again.

Walking to her car in a pair of heels that were fit for a girl half her height, a diamond bracelet her grandmother had said was a gift from her mother but had actually purchased herself, she tried not to think about how pale her legs probably looked. She wasn't oblivious to her sex appeal, but she didn't like dresses, or anything that was comparatively lacking in comfort. If she could have gotten away with jeans and a hoodie she would have. But her Em-clothing was in the car, and it would be just a few hours before she could peel this shit off.

Emily was always early to everything in those days, partly because she was nothing if not punctual, but mostly because she didn't have anything better to do. Except read. Which she would most definitely trade for dinner.

Regretfully, past a few twists and turns through lobby men and various haphazardly placed bars, Emily walked into a Mia-less dining room. Her family members and their respective significant others were there, staring her up and down as if she were an alien on display.

Hi, Emily forced out through her constricted chest. She didn't breathe. I'm Emily, Mia's—

Happy Birthday. Emily's eyes twitched before she focused on the speaker. Emily felt her head tilt so far to the right that her ear was resting on her shoulder, but she couldn't stop it. The woman had the kind of beauty Emily would be attracted to if she was romantically into women. She had some of Mia's features, yes, but she was so much prettier. She was so much more than the societal standard that was Mia. She had skin that glowed under the dim lights and silky dark hair, and she wore her black dress with class though she was not thin by any stretch of the word. She was so beautiful.

We were in the car, the woman said, when Mia left your birthday message.

Thank you, Emily nodded slightly, taking a seat at the long table.

So you're the *friend*, another woman said sarcastically, dark eye shadow plastered over her eyes and collagen practically leaking out of her lips. She began to drill Emily on what she did, and how she knew Mia. She was obviously another one of Mia's siblings, and she was obviously a major bitch.

Emily closed her eyes, gulping down a monster of a breath as the room began to spin. She never did like that ride at the carnival that spun so quickly that you were slammed against the wall as the floor began to drop, and this was no different. She clutched the edge of the dining table for support. Voices of The Shadow started in deliberately, whispering in both ears as his voice filled her head like a thick, dark cloud and overpowered the voices of the people sitting next to her. Emily knew this situation all too well and, as the man's foreign language escalated and began to screech at her, she reminded herself that from the outside, all she was, was a woman sitting at a table with her eyes closed. She didn't make a sound; she didn't move. She was no different than someone falling into meditation in public. Though, that wasn't necessarily normal either. But if she had been reacting like she should to a situation such as this one, someone would have already called the police. She could regain control over this situation, if she was quick about it.

His growls came from a lightless world that was not her own. Her instinct was to twitch as he snarled right next to her ear, to back herself into a corner of the elegant room and force her head between her legs until it stopped, but she couldn't do that. Not here.

She opened her eyes. A twister of harsh wind filled the restaurant, slapping her hair across her face. It hit her dead on, and a bang crashed just where she was sitting, it would seem, like a bomb had exploded in her head. The harsh sound signaling the release of the creatures from their undefined prison, birds with harsh lines for wings the color of cream corn filled the elegant room, squawking like crows. Emily closed her eyes, breathing through her nose, and her eyes popped open again, without warning, as if she were a member of the undead.

Before her lay the scene that she had walked into ten minutes before. An undisturbed room set for a wedding celebration. Save for the ten people who were staring at her as if she were an alien. Emily smiled and calmly forced her hand upwards. Her fingertips grazed her forehead.

Migraine, she said sweetly.

Mia's presence with her new husband saved her then as she entered in a wedding dress and a smile appropriate for a queen.

Happy Birthday, she said, and they ate lemon-roasted chicken.

*   *   *

Emily would have liked to blame anti-social behavior for her decision to leave the reception before anyone else, but she knew very well that was not the case.

The blatant lie that was the current essence of Emily (appearing when she surrounded herself with those who she didn't undoubtedly trust with her life)—the beautiful young woman who was elegantly social; quiet yet politely engaging—lasted for three hours, and she'd had enough.

She rounded the room to hug the bride goodbye, and discretely, under the table, Mia handed her a bag laden with glitter. Inside was a small book that, in black-and-white photos, told the story of Pedro, the angst-ridden cat.

Emily couldn't ever remember laughing so hard in her entire life.

Are you going to see him? Mia asked her.

Emily's face couldn't look more shocked if someone had used human blood to paint her skin red. See who? she asked incredulously.

Whoever is taking so much of your time lately.

Emily couldn't be that surprised that Mia had noticed. Saturday morning phone conversations were a bit of a ritual for the best friends, and suddenly, Friday evening tended to be Brendan-time more often than not. If he was in her bed the next morning, the phone wasn't getting answered.

Something like that, Emily said.

CHAPTER TWELVE

HAVING TRADED HER ELEGANT DRESS for faded jeans and a hoodie with a Bukowski quote on it in one of the hotel bathrooms, Emily texted Brendan from the car.

Birthday wedding accomplishment unlocked. You still want to have a drink?

The reply didn't come until six hours later, at approximately four in the morning, at which time Brendan wished Emily a happy birthday (even though it was technically no longer her birthday) and informed her that he was so drunk, he was considering sleeping on the sidewalk.

This was of course after Emily declined to spend what was left of her birthday with Ada.

Emily rolled out of bed, where she had been staring at the ceiling since she arrived home, and called him.

Tell me where you are, she said.

At *Shore,* he sighed.

Stay there. I'll be there in ten minutes.

*   *   *

Brendan only halfway lied. He was lying on the sidewalk in front of *Shore,* but he wasn't sleeping. He could feel Will's presence on the curb next to him, but he wasn't saying anything. That was the beauty of their friendship. Will understood Brendan.

No one really understood Brendan, but more than anyone, Will did.

Her cool hand felt wonderful against his skin as it slipped in between the concrete and his neck. She squeezed. It sent a soothing chill through his body.

"Let me take you home," she whispered.

"I don't want to go home," he heard his voice float into the air. Miraculously, she helped him get up—how could little Emily be so strong?—and into her car. He lay with his eyes closed in the passenger seat, albeit awake, as she drove him to her house. The world spinning, he managed to walk himself into her house and fall not on the floor but on her couch. She removed his shoes, and he begged her to come to him, holding his arms out to her.

She crawled on top of him, nuzzling her head into his neck. Beating against his, her heart threatened to tear its way out of her chest. He didn't bother asking her about Mia's wedding; obviously it wasn't an ideal evening. It was her fucking birthday. And he definitely didn't attempt any activity that would possibly arouse her. That wasn't happening tonight. There was no way he would survive it. He gently pressed his lips against her forehead, and her breaths began to slow. Somewhere between this world and the land of his familiar dreamless sleep, he said something that he wouldn't remember.

"I'm an asshole," his voice said. "I'm sorry."

He would forget what he said, but Emily wouldn't. Because Emily wouldn't have forgiven him for that night as easily as she had if she had been asleep in that moment like he thought she had. But Emily wasn't asleep. Emily was never asleep. Emily would forgive him then, and forgive him for every fucked up thing he ever did to her, and every horrible way in which he treated her, because she was Emily, and he was Brendan. Maybe, just maybe, there was someone in the world that understood Brendan Tanner better than Will, after all.

*   *   *

Since she'd broken up with Seth, Emily found herself spending more time with Kat, Ada, and inevitably, Mia. Mia still hadn't been to Emily's house, due to her no-people policy (except Brendan, of course), but Emily was at Mia's new place once a week at least, if not more.

Mia's new husband, Andrew, was like Emily in at least one way: he was not who everyone thought he was. The sweet, charming man that whispered sweet nothings in Mia's ear at the dinner table at their wedding was a façade. That man didn't exist. Her husband was a cruel, verbally and physically abusive human being. Nothing was good enough—not dinner, not the fact that she made more money than him and paid all the bills, and when she made him angry, he hurt her and played it off like it was her fault.

Mia didn't really want to talk about that in any serious way, so, with wine on the curb outside her beach apartment, Emily talked and smoked and Mia listened as well as Mia could listen. She was the kind of girl who should wear that shirt that says *I don't mean to interrupt but I think of something and then I get excited.* For hours, Emily told Mia of her antithesis of a life with Brendan—everything but his name—and Mia hugged her in all the right places.

Who is he? Mia asked.

Just a guy.

Why won't you tell me his name?

Because if I do that will make it too real.

Mia eyed her. What letter?

Emily laughed sardonically. How old are we, five?

Mia's persistence journeyed on. You're not telling me if I guess. And you can't very well lie to me. What letter?

Emily rolled her eyes. B. She wasn't worried. Mia hadn't stuck around long enough to watch what had occurred between Emily and Brendan at the show, and she didn't talk to anyone on a regular basis who had.

B . . . Bryan . . . Br . . . Oh my . . . Emily! Mia squealed.

This wasn't going to go well.

You're fucking Brendan?!

Emily let her head fall in her lap and her alcohol-ridden mind told her to laugh, so she did.

I sort of knew, Mia said, somewhere, in the back of my mind, I knew it was him.

Emily turned her head to Mia, laying her cheek on her knee.

He's really hot, Mia said.

Yeah, Emily sighed.

Do you love him?

Yes.

She nodded. You guys would be so cute together. Gorgeous babies.

The depths in which Emily thought this conversation was headed disappeared from view. Emily laughed. Oh, shut the fuck up, Mia.

I'm *just* saying.

*   *   *

Mia gave a friend of hers—some douche named Renaud—Emily's number. He owned like six businesses and was rich and drove an Audi, or something. He had lost a lot of weight recently and was in the market for a trophy wife, apparently. It was Emily's first run-in with the fact that Mia had no idea what kind of person she was, or she didn't care. Which it was, Emily couldn't decide.

Mia maintained the ideal that there was absolutely nothing wrong with dating or having sexual relationships with more than one guy at a time, as she had done it before she was married, several times, which was inevitably the defining factor for her giving Emily's number to a stranger.

They talked on the phone, and by the third call, he was already correcting her incessant use of profanity. That should have been the first and last straw, but he wanted to take her out to dinner, and she had nothing particularly better to do that night, so she went.

Based on his financial situation, Emily expected a ritzy restaurant to which she had to dress up, but he ended up taking her to some franchise Chinese cuisine place, which was fine with her. She wore red jeans that no longer fit her—one of the unfavorable side effects of anti-psychotic drugs is weight gain and she had lost it all—and her favorite white sweater. When she arrived, he lectured her about her driving 'like a bat out of hell' through a parking lot. He talked about himself the entire time, which was also fine with her. He was rich and he was old—in the mental sense, not the physical—and he was boring, and the second they exited the restaurant, she told him to never call her again.

The microwave clock's bright green 11:59 alerted her to the end of yet another day when she arrived home, and as it struck midnight in a strikingly modern way, she realized that it was Brendan's birthday.

Happy Birthday, she texted him.

She had a reply within minutes.

Yay! Thank youuuu! What are you doing?

Just got home from dinner with a friend.

Wanna come hang out? It's still early. Come to Shore!

Okay, she replied, and she went to *Shore.* It was such a simple gesture, come hang out with us or whatever. But not too simple to signify the beginning of the shift of Emily's entire life from *Poor Crazy Girl* to *Schizophrenia, You Can Go Fuck Yourself*. But first, Brendan.

*   *   *

She looked really beautiful tonight.

Brendan stared at her over his smile as she walked in. She was wearing these red skinny jeans, and this tunic thing, with a bunch of long, dangly necklaces and bracelets with peace signs on them. Her eyes were lined with just the right amount of makeup to make the violet in her eyes pop under the dim lights of the bar. Those eyes found him, and he leaped forward and wrapped her in his arms. He felt her every muscle relax under his touch. He kissed the top of her head.

"Happy Birthday," she smiled, and it wasn't one of *those* smiles, the ones she gave everyone else. It was a real, real Em smile. They were few and far between, and Bren got lost in the moment of it so he could remember it later.

"Let me buy you a drink," he said finally.

"It's your birthday! Let me buy *you* a drink. Let me buy you ten."

Brendan laughed. "Well, all right, I guess that would be okay."

CHAPTER THIRTEEN

HE ENDED UP GETTING HER DRUNK after all. Brendan couldn't really ever remember seeing Emily so drunk that her filter was all the way off, but based upon the Emily that was with him tonight—the one he knew was in there somewhere—he figured that was a safe bet. She was on her third drink, and they were basically leaving, but he wouldn't let her walk out until she finished the one she had in her hand. She was slurping her straw with that weird kind of smile that is only in the eyes, because a girl cannot really smile with a straw in her mouth, and then her knees started to bend, and she slowly lowered herself to the floor, as if she could make her drink disappear by making herself disappear. He was laughing, and she was sort of silently laughing, and then she was really laughing, and she took a deep breath and shoved the tall glass at Will's chest, a quarter of clear gin left in it.

"You did well, Grasshopper," Will said, halfway smirking as much as Will ever halfway smirked, and he tossed the rest of it back. "I have a *Starburst*," he said, setting the drink down. His mouth puckered. "It tastes weird now."

"What color *Starburst*?" Emily asked, widening her eyes like a little girl might at the mention of candy.

"I dunno," Will said.

"So how do you know what color blue is if you don't even know what color *Starburst* is in your fucking mouth?"

Will's mouth straightened into a flat line in his best attempt at holding back his laugh. Brendan didn't bother, though. His stomach hurt, he laughed so hard. Straightening himself from the humor that practically tore him in two, he watched Will, smiling at Emily, and Emily, with her head tilted to the side, like an amused puppy.

Brendan left them there, trading that insufferable moment for the social butterfly that he was and he joined his friends at the bar.

They eventually stumbled through crowded streets and deserted back-way alleys, Brendan's hands on her waist to hold her up, his lips on her neck to keep her awake. He was telling her how he ran into Mia today and she came onto him, like literally grabbed his ass and whispered a giggle in his ear, like she had the first time which is why he ended their friendship, because Mia only wanted attention until she got it. He was telling her this whole story, and at one point Emily stopped laughing for a minute, but then he kissed her and he didn't care because she was laughing again, and Emily and Brendan and Will and the California night with haphazardly decorated stars was just sort of perfect.

He got her coffee at some place—he didn't even know—and he lost her in cigarette smoke and conversations with his friends at a place he'd never been to. It had been hours since he'd seen her—two at least—and he looked up, and she was ten feet away, talking with Frank. He was very animated, tugging at his shirt and waving his hands like those guys with the orange cones that guided the planes in and out of the airport. He totally would have known what they were called if he wasn't this royally drunk, and though he would never admit it out loud, he knew in that moment that a girl like Emily would be the only kind of girl he could ever give himself exclusively to, because he didn't have to babysit her. Brendan never had to worry about Emily. Unlike Every Woman in the History of the Universe, Emily could take care of her fucking self. That would be the only time Brendan would entertain this kind of thinking though. Although he'd metaphorically admitted to himself that he was in love with Emily Colt, he wouldn't even remember it ever happened. Because Emily was drunk, and Brendan was drunk, and that was the only time either of them were this happy. With each other, that is.

*   *   *

They didn't disappear into a fog of a bedroom right away. They ate fast food breakfast in her car in the dark and smoked a lot of cigarettes (not in the car of course), and he drove her home because he was the less-drunk of the two drunks. She lay back, reclined in her seat, and he didn't even know if she was listening when he told her about Will.

"He met this girl, Jocelyn, at *Shore* one night, you know, years ago when we first started out. She was this flame of a girl, with big red hair and a mouth like, like you actually." Brendan laughed. "They dated a while, not long enough, but whatever. Anyway she got pregnant, and Will and Jocelyn had a son. His name was Connor. He was the most beautiful little boy with Will's hair and these shocking ocean-blue eyes, god, Em, I stared into those eyes of his for hours. Will was going to marry this girl, he was going to buy her a house and get another job and quit the band; he would have given her the world, I promise you. Just when he was ready, she started to change. She was quiet and broken and really, really thin. She had stopped eating. The sexual end of their relationship was over. On Connor's first birthday, at his party, Will went looking for Joss when she had disappeared, and he found her shooting up in the bathroom. Fucking heroin. He told me that the lower part of her arm was practically black. He lost it; he hit her, so enraged that she could be so stupid, that she could put their son in danger. When Will woke up the next morning, Jocelyn and Connor were gone.

"We searched for weeks: the police, the FBI, we even hired a private investigator. Nothing. Until two weeks later, they found their rotting bodies in an abandoned house up north. Jocelyn had overdosed, and whoever she was with had slit the baby's throat. For what reason, Will or I never found out."

Emily's deep breaths filled the small car, and Brendan realized she was in fact listening.

"Why are you telling me this?" she whispered with her eyes closed.

"Because you have something with him."

She turned her head towards him in the driver's seat, her violet eyes sparkling at him. He would think their vibrancy would dull under a film of drunkenness, but no such luck.

"I don't know what that means," she said.

"I don't know either. Your connection with my best friend is undeniable, though. Frank explained it best to me once. He said that every conversation you two have is like a dance. He told me that when you two are together he tunes out your voices and just watches you, watches your energies battle one another. It fascinates him."

"Is that why you always walk away when I talk to him?"

Brendan stared at the road. He wasn't aware that she had noticed.

"No," he said finally.

"Why, then?"

"Because I don't want my friends to fall in love with you," he blurted, regretting it immediately, but pushed on. "And I refuse to entertain you and Will."

She laughed freely. "You mean like you fell in love with me? Why? Because their affection will make what you're about to do that much harder?"

"Look," he smiled at her forcefully. "We're here," he said, pulling into Emily's driveway.

Ignoring him, she said, "Too late."

*   *   *

He took his time with her. He had to give her that, at least. He had to give her everything he had to give, for tonight. He was unfazed by their adventitious conversation in the car. He kissed her deliberately in the living room. In the hallway, on the way to her bedroom, he was three-fingers deep inside her euphoria. On her bed, his hand was around the back of her neck, tangled in her hair, his other hand on her face. His rhythm was not a death-metal classic, but it was modern. It was the sound of something never heard before inside Emily's house. It was the sound of no sound at all, yet lyrics rang in and out of his ears. They were a melody, *the* melody, and she came, oh god, Emily came so many times; the whole thing was just impossible.

He fucked her, Jesus Christ he fucked her, for hours, and hours, and hours. And then it was all over.

*   *   *

They slept the day away. Her memories from the night before came in flashes, and she was sure there was something missing.

On the balcony of Emily's upstairs loft, they talked with the sun setting in their eyes. For four hours, they smoked and they talked, of Will, of radio waves and fireworks and the FDA's conspiracy to keep the pharmaceutical companies alive. That was when Brendan must have figured out there was something wrong with Emily's brain. A moment wherein she knew nearly everything there was to know about the subject of mental illness and its prescribed medication, when she didn't seem to know anything else about the world around her. That must have been the moment, because that day, Brendan would say goodbye to Emily. Without actually ever saying goodbye.

She drove him to his car, and he didn't immediately hug her and get out like he always did. He did something else.

I think this . . . thing—I think it's time it ended, Emily. I feel like you want something from me that I won't ever be able to provide.

She didn't bother fighting him on it. I disagree, but I respect your decision, she said.

Thank you, he said, and he got out of the car.

Emily didn't cry. She didn't watch his stupid sexy body float away from her forever. She didn't care anymore. She didn't care about anything. Her existence was numb.

Fuck you, Brendan Tanner. Fuck you.

CHAPTER FOURTEEN

EMILY WOKE TO SHADOWS and their voices. They looked different today, because the entire world hurt. The numbness had worn off sometime between sleep and awake, and she was seeing red. The shadows on the walls were not shadows at all, but red blobs consisting of teeth and claws. Her house reeked of pain.

The whole world was fucking bleeding.

She tugged at her hair, looking down at her body. Even her skin was red. He had done a number on her; her hips were scratched up and her inner thighs were tender and bruised.

Her pillow still smelled like him.

She got up and eventually found herself at a massage parlor down the street from *Danielle's*. She lay bare on her stomach, a towel over her ass, waiting. The sound of the door made her close her eyes, and she tried to tune out the soft music that started playing, to no avail. As her body began to relax under the touch of the soft hands above her, she lost it. She lost her shit; she lost everything.

The therapist would not know the difference unless she had an advanced sense of salt smell. Emily didn't do the ugly cry thing. She had learned how to carry herself as a sad, damaged girl from years of experience. She was very good at it; Emily Colt could cry in a room full of people and no one would ever know.

People see what they want to see.

Emily didn't remember getting from the parlor to the bookstore. But it didn't matter. It didn't matter what she did from that moment. She was burning from the inside out faster than she could put one foot in front of the other. She was never going to see him again. Brendan was gone, and she was going to die.

Emily wouldn't survive this. There was no fucking way she would survive this.

*   *   *

Savannah was waiting by the door inside *Danielle's*, behind one of the posts where she wouldn't be visible to Emily. She caught sight of Emily through the black-trimmed windows, and she looked like a ghost or a zombie. Whatever was worse than both of those. A zombie-ghost. Through the window, Emily dragged her feet across the asphalt, each step looking like her last. Savannah didn't think she'd successfully make it inside, but Emily was too stubborn to let Savannah help her if she'd gone outside, so Savannah just waited. Emily did eventually make it in, the door falling shut behind her right before she collapsed. Right next to the post.

"I gotchya," Savannah sang to her unconscious boss as she lay half-dead in her arms. "A fucking man is not going to take away everything you have achieved. Don't worry, Em. Everything's going to be okay."

Savannah giggled, carrying Emily to the couch in her office. Did she just say the F-word?

*   *   *

"Why aren't you my bestie?"

Savannah laughed her infectious girlie laugh from somewhere near.

"Because Mia is your bestie. Also: you just said bestie."

"Not anymore," something resembling Emily's voice said, ignoring Savannah's latter comment. The memory of Brendan's admission about her supposed best friend surfaced, but for some reason, she didn't care.

Emily opened her eyes. Her bookstore was every book lover's dream. Plush orange chairs cornered black leather couches in the large open space that was only lit by the sun raying through the windows. There were no traditional bookstore stacks. There were a few shelves here and there against the walls, but mostly there were just books. Books in cubes, books on tables next to vintage coffee makers, books stacked on the floor. It was all very haphazard and unorganized. It was all very perfect.

"Who are you?" Emily eventually slurred out at the forty-something woman standing at her feet.

Savannah piped in from where she sat next to her on the floor. Her hand was cool in Emily's.

"This is my friend Nancy," Savannah said. "The Chakra Lady."

"The who-what?" Emily widened her eyes.

Nancy smiled. "Your energy is very strong, Emily." Emily's body seemed to have been gently kissed by a wave of electricity at the word 'energy.' Emily smiled. She couldn't feel her legs. "Your energy took over the second I started pulling at your chakras."

"Pulling *what*?"

"I'll explain later," Savannah interjected. "Frank is on his way."

Emily's head fell to the side and she looked up at Savannah's perfectly even face. "You called him?" she whispered.

"Who, Brendan? Fuck no."

"Savannah," Emily laughed, "did you just say the F-word?"

*   *   *

After Nancy left Emily was practically immobilized—immobilized in a good way though, like the feeling you got when the sheets of your bed cocooned you, protecting you from the stress of the day—there was a knock at the door. Savannah apparently had taken it upon herself to close the shop for the day. Which was probably a good idea.

Savannah jumped up from the couch in Emily's office to answer it. Emily called her back, and she paused at the door, swooping around so that her blonde hair swayed in a circle as she spun.

"How did you get Frank's number?"

"It was in your phone. I remember you mentioning his name."

"How did it get there?" Emily asked the room, not expecting an answer. "He never gave me his number."

"I don't know," Savannah whispered, and she disappeared.

She returned with Frank on her heels. "Emily," he breathed, "how are you?"

"Um," she said, as way of an answer.

"Lie down," he said.

"What?"

"Lie down," he said, pointing to the couch she sat on. "Lie down and close your eyes."

Reluctantly, she did what was asked of her.

"Don't leave, Sav," Emily begged blindly.

"I won't," she said quietly.

"Empty your mind," Frank's voice said next to her. "Make it a black hole. No thoughts. No memories. Just emptiness. Breathe. As you inhale, imagine the breath filling your head. Exhale, it's getting released. Everything that ails you: let it go through your breaths, push it all out."

It was easy.

"Remove everything about the world. No people, no objects, no world. Everything is dark. You are floating in a starless sky."

Electricity moved in a gentle wave just over the surface of her skin. An aura of sedation swallowed her. She couldn't feel anything; she felt everything.

Her limbs went limp, her muscles mush. A smile tugged at her lips. She lazily opened her eyes. Frank was smiling down at her.

"You need to eat better," he said. "Lots of greens. Get off the dairy and the bread. Protein." He dropped a bag of various bottles in her lap. "Take these."

"What are they?"

"Supplements. And vodka."

"What does the vodka do?"

"Vodka fixes everything," he said. "I'll see you soon."

"Frank?"

"Yes, Emily?"

"Will you tell him you were here?"

"No. No, I won't. Ever."

"Thank you," Emily breathed.

"Emily?"

"Yes?"

"It's your ankles putting too much pressure on your feet. Wear better shoes. Soak them. And get more massages."

"Foot massages?"

"No. Just more regular massages."

"Why?"

"Because you deserve it."

*   *   *

Halfway through the customer-less day, another knock came at the door. Emily was up and moving around, bustling from book to book, sometimes napping on the floor with an open book covering her face. From the opposite side of the store, where they kept the YA books, Savannah sang Ellie Goulding songs.

"I'll get it!" she chimed and danced gracefully over to the door.

Emily wasted no time dropping the book in her hand and running to him the second she saw him. She held his broken face in front of her, sadness baking him red.

"What are you doing here?! How did you . . ."

"I lost my job," he piped in. "Got kicked out of my house. I got a place with some friends."

Derek. He had moved away several years before, and in all that time, Emily hadn't seen or heard from her kid brother. And now he was back. She wrapped him in another hug.

"It's so good to see you."

"You too, Emmy. I wanted to see if you wanted to go out with me and my friends tonight," he said, smiling. "To the gay club girrrrrrl."

"Why the hell do you want to take your ancient sister out with you and your gay friends?"

He smiled. *"Because you`re beautiful . . . "*

Emily nodded, smiling. Okay, she agreed.

Okay, he said, and they laughed.

CHAPTER FIFTEEN

NO ONE EMILY KNEW PERSONALLY ever came to the shop, but today was a special day, apparently. Mia showed up a couple minutes after Derek left. At the sight of her, Emily's face felt like your hand would if you closed it around a hot coal. She picked up a hardcover of *Gatsby* from the table, snarled you fucking whore, and bashed Mia as hard as she could on the side of her head.

Emily blinked as her world started to shake, like an earthquake. It stopped just after a moment, and she found herself standing in the same spot she was before she picked up the book from the table. She looked up and found Mia in the doorway, where she had been the whole time.

For the first time in her life, she really wished that hadn't been a hallucination.

Not a good time, Emily said simply.

Mia giggled, pushing her curls back. Not a good time for your sista from another mista?

Get the fuck out of my store, Mia, Emily said, and Mia looked revolted, stepping back as if Emily really had hit her with a book. And don't ever come back. If you do, I will beat the living shit out of you.

Emily . . . ?

I told you that I loved him, Mia, Emily said, tears streaming down her face. *I told you that I loved him.*

I was just—

You were just being a whore, Emily said calmly. You were just being you.

As if to agree, not one mark of emotion anywhere on her face, Mia turned and left. That was the last time Emily ever saw Mia Molera. Eventually, there would be no more toxic souls left in Emily's life, starting with her.

Mostly because they all died. Emily could safely say that only one of those deaths was her fault, though.

*   *   *

She wore the red dress.

Like with all planned outings, Emily wished she hadn't agreed to go, though for different reasons. Her brother was young—young enough to need a fake ID—and his friends were young and dumb, and because they were young, they were irresponsible and annoying drunks.

Derek's new place wasn't far from downtown, so he, Emily, and his not-lesbian friend Fiona, walked amongst a crowd of night-crawlers. With her phone, Emily took a picture of one girl's ass, because it was in booty shorts and it was nice. Next to her, a girl she didn't know laughed as her camera flashed.

Emily had been to the club before. The company was cheap and the drinks were expensive. The walls were lined with platforms for the male dancers dressed in nothing but speedo-type underwear. There was a lower level that was used for dancing, and the bar was on the upper level, below a giant glowing orange light thing that looked like a friendly spider, if such a thing existed. Outside, on the patio, was one female dancer in a leather bikini. Of the entertainers, she made three times as much as anyone else. A few feet away from where men and women crowded around her, sticking cash beneath her strings, was a patio area with tables and smokers. This is where Emily liked to hang out at this place, and tonight was no different.

What surprised her though was that Fiona did not get lost on the dance floor with Derek, but followed her outside, with two clear drinks in her hand.

"Go dance!" Emily waved at her. "I'm fine, I promise you."

"I'm good," she smiled the most genuine smile and sat at a table with Emily, pushing one of the drinks over.

"Excuse me," a bald man tapped Emily on the shoulder. "I don't mean to be rude but I just have to tell you, you are so beautiful." He raised his hands to the sky. "You glow under the stars."

Emily laughed nervously. "Um, thank you."

He smiled at her, turning back to his friends.

Fiona and Emily laughed together. It would turn out that nineteen-year-old Fiona was not dumb, or irresponsible, or an annoying drunk. Fiona Harvey was really, really smart. They spoke of books, illness, American troops, and of politics. They peed at a park behind the club, squatting against a brick wall for support.

Derek met some Polish rapper and went home with him in his Mercedes. Fiona took a picture of the guy's driver's license.

They stumbled back to the house, collapsing on Derek's couches, laughing way too loudly for what was considered acceptable at three o'clock in the morning.

Scrambled eggs woke Emily sometime around noon, and over coffee, she and Fiona talked shit about mainstream coffee chains.

Emily seemed to remember a phone call just before she fell asleep, a familiar voice saying that he was sorry through the speaker. *Don't be mad at me*, the words rang in her head. But that couldn't be. Emily was really drunk. She must have blacked out or something. Or, she was just, you know, schizophrenic. Either way.

*   *   *

Over time, Emily stole Fiona away from Derek. Emily tried to hang out with him—both girls did—but he was so negative. Derek loved to play the flaming gay card and in the public eye, he was the most wonderful person to be around; Emily never laughed as much as she laughed with him. But the antithesis that was Derek these days, well. His childhood had broken him. He believed that no one loved him and that everyone owed him something. He pushed away everything that was wonderful or had positive potential. When he spoke, all Emily heard was her mother. He hated her; Derek's hatred for Karla burned a hole through his chest and through his head. But sometimes people were just mirrors, and Karla, she was a mirror of Derek's existence. He was exactly like her. Both Karla and Derek got to the point where they would call one another and yell, cuss the other out until they couldn't speak or breathe anymore, and then they would call Emily and tell her how awful the other was. Karla was a terrible mother, and Derek was an even more terrible son. And the truth was that Emily didn't want to hear it anymore. From either of them.

She stopped replying to Derek's texts and didn't answer the phone when Karla called (her mother didn't know how to text). When she finally agreed to hang out with him again, and they got really drunk, Derek said something to Emily that she would never forget. He told her that he didn't care if she loved him, because it would never be good enough. Quietly, she cried, and she left him standing there on the street. When Fiona found out what he had said to her, she refused to speak to Derek ever again. She told Emily that she was a good sister and a good person and that Derek didn't deserve her.

He called a few weeks later, saying that no one would help him, and that he wanted to sleep away his life. He told her that he wanted to die.

"You should call the police, if that's the case," Emily said.

"Emily, shut the fuck up, you make it sound like I would kill myself. You know better than that."

He was crying.

"So what do you want, Derek?"

"I want you to tell me what to do!"

"What to do with life? Get out of bed, Derek. That's what you do. You get out of bed, and you get yourself a cup of fucking coffee. That's all you can do."

He hung up on her.

*   *   *

The threesome-friendship Emily had with Fiona and Savannah felt like a movie set in New York City more often than not. Fiona taught Savannah how to smoke pot properly, and Emily explained to both of them that she called Fiona a not-lesbian because she walked the earth shouting lesbian, yet Emily believed she was one of those who could be in a relationship with anybody. It was about the human connection for

Fiona; not the label stuck to the outside of it. Savannah was always making fun of Emily, teasing her for secretly being in love with Fiona.

Emily would laugh. "Nah, Fiona's not into girls like me, she would say."

"Why not?"

"Because," she winked, "Fiona wants a military spouse. You know, so she can reap the benefits."

Savannah would laugh, and they'd go back to their books.

*   *   *

Time passed. Wounds healed. Emily wasn't about to say that she wasn't in love with Brendan anymore because she would be lying. But it was a soft kind of love. The kind that lined the edges of your heart, instead of filling it. In time, she forgave him because in reality, he really never did anything wrong. He had been up front with her, and she chose not to hear what he was saying. It takes two to tango, and if you dance too long, implosion is inevitable.

Emily used meditation and holistic healing to her advantage. Her monthly visits with Frank consisted of old cartoons with no dialogue and French fashion shows. He brought her books that he knew she'd never buy for the store because they would never sell. He told her stories of his years. He never mentioned Brendan. Neither did she. She didn't go back to *Shore*, and she found other music to listen to.

Jace was no longer a distant friend. He called her one night to randomly say hello, and they talked for hours every night after that. Sometimes they would fall asleep on the phone. They talked about books and art and comics, about everything that was wrong with the world, about feminism, about girls with tattoos. They talked about being roommates somewhere cold. They talked about coffee.

And when she wasn't talking to Jace, Emily read. She did a lot of research. She learned that healing the mind starts with the body. The voices, the hallucinations, they never left, but they waned. They had somehow traveled to the other side of the locked door, sucked through the cracks, and they couldn't get back in. She shut out her own illness and by doing that, it danced away from her. Soon, she didn't need Frank anymore. She spent her time on girls' nights with Fiona and Savannah.

She read a lot of books. She started a book blog, wherein she earned thousands of followers in just six months. She learned how to *tweet*. She hosted author events at the store. She traded her hoodies for vintage sweaters and her tennis shoes for flip flops. She got pedicures. She drank wine. She laughed at hipsters. The whole thing was like having perfect hair: you never have a bad day, and you always feel beautiful.

She was sexually deprived, but Emily could never have sex with anyone she didn't trust, so she tried to get past it, and when she couldn't, she bought the world's first laser vibrator. And that was the end of that frustration.

The only thing Emily worried about nearly a year after she had sworn to herself that she was dead inside, was spending Christmas alone, and whether or not that made her a loser.

That was the thing about an American Christmas, though. The whole point was to give gifts and to receive them.

*   *   *

Emily's older, half-brother Justin surprised her on Christmas Eve. He had been absent most of her life because he'd lived with her father, but they had the kind of relationship wherein they didn't have to talk for five years and he would just show up and they'd be as close as best friends would be on any given day.

Emily didn't have a Christmas tree—it was her experience that Iver would knock it over—but Justin brought gifts and chocolate, and that was more than enough. Justin didn't drink alcohol, so Emily made coffee. He knew about her Schizophrenia through their father, but he never mentioned it, not even tonight. His carpenter business was booming, and he told her that he was making her a bookcase. It was a good thing, because she was out of book-space, and he had given her some antique books he had found at a shop in LA.

He left around eleven, and Emily grabbed a book, preparing herself to stay up another hour to wish Savannah a Merry Christmas. Her phone, however, went off long before she expected it to.

But it wasn't Savannah.

Merry Christmas the text said.

She looked at the tiny square photo attached to the contact in the top left corner. She wondered if he still looked the same as he did when Will took that photo with her phone when Brendan wasn't looking. He was smiling, staring off into the distance. Emily wasn't in the photo, so she wondered if he had been looking at her with the calm eyes that stared back at her now.

Same to you, she texted back.

How are you?

Good! And yourself?

Wonderful. What's new in Emily's world?

Oh, you know. Just living the dream.

Haha, he said back. *Well. I have a new house. And a new bed. Wanna see?*

Okay, she said, and she followed texted directions to Brendan's new house. Will didn't live there, and that made Emily sad. Not because there was a possibility that Brendan and Will weren't as good of friends as they had once been, but because Will wasn't there.

She missed him.

CHAPTER SIXTEEN

SHE WAS SO BEAUTIFUL. Even in the dark. With no light to tell him what she looked like, she was stunning. She had on these tight dark jeans with knee high boots over them, a dark brown leather jacket over the white tank top that barely covered her cleavage. She still didn't have any makeup on, but she didn't need it. The violet in her eyes sparkled at him as he swooped her in for a hug.

"Hi," he whispered in her ear.

She giggled. Brendan had never heard Emily giggle before. "Hiiiii," she whispered back, her hands spider-crawling up his neck and into his hair, where her fingers squeezed his scalp gently.

Brendan shivered.

"I've missed you so much, Em," he heard himself say in a gentle breeze of a breath.

"Yeah, me too," she said into his shoulder. She was shaking. She inhaled a deep breath. "This beach weather is ridiculous."

Brendan laughed. They went inside and drank beer in the dark. He liked listening to her talk. When she spoke of what she had been up to, of her bookstore, she tilted her head back when she laughed, or sometimes ran her fingers through her hair. She never mentioned Mia.

Good. Emily was better off.

Mid-sentence about someone named Fiona, Emily stopped talking, because Brendan was kissing her, and he was carrying her to his room, with her booted legs wrapped tightly around his waist, and he practically came before he got his pants off. He would have liked to say that he fucked her all night to make up for lost time, but that's just not what happened. Their connection that night was a harmonic one, with melodies backing it up. He kissed her, and he looked at her, and he kissed her again, and bit her shoulder, and held onto her tighter than he could ever remember holding on to anything when it was over and he groaned in her ear. He never groaned. Brendan was soundless through sex. Except this time.

She slept in his arms, and when she woke up and moved to get dressed and leave just like he used to leave, he said, "You don't have to leave."

She said, "Okay," and on Christmas morning, they watched *Frozen*.

* * *

"He smells like sex. That's what it is! It's why *ALL THE WOMEN* are attracted to him. It's in my hair, on my clothes. I can't get away from it. The man smells like fucking . . . he smells like *fucking*, Sav! Ugh."

Savannah wasn't disappointed in Emily like she thought she'd be. She expected a lecture, *I WAS THE ONE WHO PICKED YOU UP OFF THAT FREAKING FLOOR, O.M.G., EMILY!* or something. But Savannah was mysterious in that way.

All she said was, "You sound so calm, so . . . perfect. It's amazing that one person can have that effect." She took a single discernable breath. "This is the kind of love you only find in books, Emily, and you're living it, right now."

* * *

Emily didn't expect to see him again after that Christmas night, and she was okay with that. It was a one-time thing, one last goodbye, and she preferred the positive goodbye rather than the previous one.

That, of course, was not the case.

Brendan reached out again, and again, and again. They drank, and Emily friend-argued with Will when he was there, and Frank winked at her, and they slept till noon. Brendan and Emily never got together, technically, but Emily didn't care about that anymore. She had a successful business, loyal friends, and the best strictly sexual relationship there ever was. Schizophrenia was just a thing, like having brown hair or wearing glasses. It was defining, not life changing.

Life was beautiful.

*   *   *

Derek died on a Wednesday in July.

His roommates found him in his bed, surrounded in a pool of his own blood. They called Emily before they called anyone else. Even the police.

His body was half-naked, shirtless, curled in a fetal position. His chest and back were splattered with bruises. A tooth lay on the floor next to his bed, and his nose was broken. His eyes were wide open. Upon careful inspection, Emily found both wrists slit vertically.

Something quietly skidded across the floor when Emily backed away from him. She looked behind her. Across the room was a small baggie of white powder with a calligraphic K on the front of it.

Only Karla would have designer bags for her drugs.

She didn't bother picking it up. The entire scene was obviously staged and the police would know that. Emily had believed her brother when he said that he would never kill himself. And he wouldn't. Quitting was not an option for this fucking family. But none of it mattered, because they would never find the killer. The killer, when fueled by her drugs, was the best disappearing act the world had ever known.

Derek Gillian's mother brought him into this broken world, and she made sure to break him of it before she took him out.

Call the police, Emily said. Tell them your roommate has been murdered.

*   *   *

The voices had gotten back inside. Someone had unlocked the door and left it open and all of them were rushing in. The ones from the nights Emily had protected Derek, the ones from when he had left her, all of them.

Her phone dead, Emily lay numbly in bed for two days, until Brendan and Will pulled her out. They brought her outside to the dark night and sat her on the curb between them. The three of them wordlessly watched fireworks, and Emily cried. Emily cried, the men on each side of her holding the pieces together. But there was no glue, and she was just a pile of broken glass, even if she was in their arms.

As the last bang in the sky went off, signaling the end of Independence Day, Emily finally looked up. Walking towards her, black-eyed and lifeless, like a star of the living dead, was her mother.

Since she was old enough to drive, she had always kept a baseball bat in her trunk. Enraged, one could always do more damage with a wooden bat than with any other weapon. Karla had taught her that. In the driveway behind her, Emily popped the trunk and removed the unused bat, still glossy from the warehouse where it had been manufactured. She walked forward, the top of the bat dragging on the ground.

She heard Will say, are you going to stop her before she does something she regrets? And then she heard Brendan say, Nope, and then the universe went black.

*   *   *

Up until that moment, after Jocelyn, after Connor, after he had trusted Brendan to keep Emily safe from herself after he asked her to keep Brendan safe, Will would definitely say that his biggest mistake in life was not stopping Emily from using that baseball bat on her mother's already lifeless body.

But that just wasn't true.

He watched the tip of the bat bounce off the fifty-something-year-old woman's hip as Emily took her first blow. Will didn't stop watching, and Emily did not stop. When Karla didn't go down, she hit her in the back of the knee, in the middle of her back, on her shoulder. Blood spattered into her violet eyes, over her sweater. On the ground, Karla moved to get up again. Brendan stepped forward and pushed her. He held her down, and Emily swung the bat behind her head and gave the last murderous blow, smashing her mother's wrinkled face in. The woman went still, and the bat fell to the ground.

The feral look that Emily's eyes transformed into was foreign to Will. She glared at him, and she turned and walked down the street.

"Let her go," Brendan said, and Will did.

And that was the biggest mistake of his life. Letting her go.

CHAPTER SEVENTEEN

EMILY DIDN'T REMEMBER the act itself, but based on the way Brendan and Will were staring at her over her mother's lifeless body, it was obvious that Emily had killed her. She wasn't surprised.

She stopped at a water fountain in someone's front yard and washed the blood off of her face. Somewhere in the middle of the street, she removed her sweater and tied her hair in a makeshift bun. She stopped by Savannah's, relieved that she wasn't home, and got the spare keys to the shop. After gathering paperwork from her office, she found herself at an airport in front of a curious woman dressed in blue.

The woman smiled at her. Where are you headed?

Emily looked down at her hands that were shaking on the white counter. Her favorite book told the story of a fiery young girl who navigated the cold, dark streets as if it were second nature. Lydia was her name.

Emily looked back up at the woman, smiling at her. Moscow.

Round-trip?

One-way, Emily clarified.

*   *   *

The voices and their dark hallucinations followed Emily on the long flight. She didn't think she slept through any of it, but it was hard to tell for sure. Her mind had reverted to the confusion between sleep and life and which was real and which was not. People on the plane politely spoke to her, but she didn't know if they existed in reality or just in her head, so she just ignored them.

When she landed, Emily faded through all of the right airport personnel at all the right times, with all the right answers. She was so good at pretending to be normal it disgusted her.

The sun was setting over elegant buildings that looked to Emily like Cinderella castles, and she watched the orange sky that was speckled with the kind of purple that she had only ever seen in her own eyes. She had been fascinated with Russian culture ever since she had read of Lydia's trials so many years before. She always thought she would visit Moscow in the winter, when the blistering cold would dare her to survive on its streets, but it was July, and it was warm. For Russia. It was warm, and it was beautiful.

It didn't really matter, though. She wouldn't survive this anyway. She had said that before, she realized, but she was not a bookstore owner anymore; she was a murderer. And that label would be stuck all over her face forever. What reasons did she have to even try anymore?

Maybe there was at least one quitter in this family.

Watching the sky turn dark, Emily walked for miles, days, it felt like, until she couldn't walk anymore. She was in sandals and her feet ached. She made it halfway across a bridge, drowned out by a bright red Cinderella castle that reminded her of Christmas. Her legs gave, and her knees made a cracking sound against the asphalt. Tears silently streamed down her cheeks. She leaned her weight on her hands, and when her arms started to shake, she let her elbows bend and her face crashed into the ground.

She saw one thing before everything went black.

Will's eyes, surrounded by the look that he gave her before she turned and walked out of her own life. It was a look she'd never seen on his face before.

He was sort of beautiful. In his own dark, depressing way, but still. She was going to miss that stupid fucking beautiful face.

*   *   *

Emily awoke after a dreamless sleep, her body warm and her head cold. She raised her hand to her head and pulled a cool cloth from her forehead. Swiping her hand across her cheek, she twitched at the tenderness and gentle scratches that came in contact with her fingertips. She opened her eyes. She was in a room lined with vintage wallpaper that must have been first designed in the nineteenth century. Beside the bed she lay in was a silk comforter fit for a queen. Under a glass chandelier was a red upholstered chair that must have cost more than her life. In it, a fierce man with scars and dents accenting his face, his blonde hair buzzed and a track suit covering his body.

Who are you? he asked in a voice from the depths of Moscow, broken with his Russian accent.

Emily Deena Colt, she breathed, her voice crackling underneath the weight of half-sleep. She didn't know how long she had been out, but it had been long enough to forget how to speak properly, apparently.

Why did you come here? Despite the accent, his English was flawless.

Why did you save me? Emily asked, tears rolling out of her eyes.

Answer my questions, he said calmly, and I will consider answering yours.

Emily gulped down her fears. This man was no common working Russian, obviously. He was going to kill her. But if that was the case, why did he save her life?

I killed someone, she said.

In America?

Yes.

Who?

Her name was Karla Gillian, Emily said. She was my mother.

The man sat back in his seat, pressing his lips together.

Why?

Because she killed my brother.

He was quiet for a long moment. That doesn't answer my question, he said eventually. Why did you come here?

To die, Emily said. She didn't hesitate. To die in peace.

He raised his head up high to really look down at her, his jaw tight. You can die here, if you like, but not in public. Not in Moscow. The last thing I need right now is a beautiful fucking American girl dead on my streets. He sighed. If you change your mind about dying in my late sister's bed, there is food in the kitchen. He got up and moved to leave the room. There is no one here, except my housekeeper. Her name is Lydia.

Emily smiled slightly before blurting, And your name?

Сергей, the man said in Russian, looking into her eyes. Sergei, in English. Sergei Melikov.

Thank you, Sergei.

There is no need to thank me. If you had not been directly threatening my life and my money, I would have left you to rot on the bridge. But you weren't, and I didn't. Sergei pressed on. You are a stupid fucking woman, Emily Colt. Just like all your kind.

I know you hate Americans, but—

I never said I hated Americans, Sergei spat. I said your kind. Women. It doesn't matter to me what country you're from. You women are fucking stupid, and I'm tired of saving you. All of you.

*   *   *

Emily ate only bread from the large plate of food, the likes of nothing she had ever seen before. She was afraid of her inability to keep anything else down. She had never been so nervous in her entire life; she was shaking.

She hadn't seen Lydia yet, but that didn't surprise her. The house she was in was monstrously stunning. She didn't know how many floors there were, but at least three, she guessed. The kitchen opened up to a hallway with diamond tile for a floor. The hallway eventually opened up to a wider hallway that served as a bridge. *The house had a fucking bridge inside.* She looked over the custom railing to find a living area below with white furniture. Above her head was a ceiling painted expertly with a map of the world. The black beams to her right towered twenty feet up with intricacy. It would take her years to explore this house. She kept going and stopped at a room wherein the sound of haphazard footsteps escaped from within. She tiptoed quietly to the open doorway and found an empty white room. On one wall hung swords and knives of all shapes and sizes. In the middle of the room, Sergei moved fluidly back and forth and in a circle, the long sword in his hand cutting the air that tried to swallow him. The top of his tracksuit was gone, replaced by only a gray tank top. He was cut, and not by knives. His arms were huge. Sergei was huge. And sexy. In a dark, dark way.

Against every instinct Emily ever had that told her to hide from the world, she stepped in. Sergei backed up, putting distance between them. He let the sword rest on his shoulder as he held it in his hand.

I know how to fight, Emily said. She cleared her throat. Not with swords, but. . . . I'm not totally useless.

He balanced the sword on two fingertips at the edge of the handle. It was perfectly balanced; a handle looking like it was made of leather, with diamond cuts in it.

Do you know what this is?

I would say a *Samurai*, Emily said, but I don't know because they are illegal in America, and I don't know anything about swords.

You killed your mother with your hands, then?

A bat, actually, she said carefully.

He laughed, his head tilting back with the boost of it. As in the kind they use in baseball?

Yes, she said, gulping her breaths down.

But you can fight, he clarified, with your hands.

Emily nodded. My ex-boyfriend taught me.

Sergei hung the sword on the wall behind him. Come here, he said quietly.

Emily stepped forward, and Sergei beat the shit out of her.

CHAPTER EIGHTEEN

SETH HAD IN FACT taught Emily how to fight. He had also taught her how to load, take apart, clean, and shoot every gun that one could buy legally and illegally in California. It was important to Seth that his woman knew how to protect herself when he wasn't around to do it for her.

But Seth wasn't in the Russian mob.

Sergei was brought in at a young age due to family ties. For most of his thirty-five years, he had killed for a living. Two years before, he had fucked with the wrong person, and his sister had been kidnapped. She was made a sex slave and raped so persistently and violently that she died. It was at her funeral that he decided he would devote the rest of his days to the sex slavery trade. To saving the—as he once called them—stupid fucking women.

Of course, the Russian mob was behind most of the sex slavery in Europe. The mob was like that, Sergei had explained. Manipulative and untrustworthy, even to its own members. Especially to its own members.

Sergei had sure trusted Emily pretty quickly. In return she'd told him about her own experience with rape in America. When she told him, he'd punched a hole in the wall.

"I told you, stupid fucking women," he'd said as she wrapped his hand.

Sergei did a little work for the mafia that he could in order to not be killed in his sleep by his own family, pushing arms in exchange for cocaine. He of course didn't do any of the work himself—he had minions for that—but he was still in charge of the guns and the drugs. And in his spare time, he had a team of ruthless nobodies with nothing to work for, whom he led to warehouses packed with battered, raped women. It was a *Robin Hood* operation in its own right: stealing for the rich to give to the poor. Or giving to the rich, in order to steal the poor from the richer.

Between in-depth conversations about Russian crime bosses and Schizophrenia at a quiet corner table in the kitchen over Rassolnik and dry bread—Sergei loved soup—Sergei taught Emily how to fight. He barely gave her time to recover from the wounds and the bruises the first time and afforded her no recovery time each time he picked her up off the ground and carried her to his bed (which was much more elegant—and comfortable—than his sister's old bed) when she couldn't get up herself.

In time, she moved like so many American actresses in ninja outfits in Hollywood. He would inevitably always beat her in a fight, but eventually it was a somewhat-fair match, and not Sergei throwing three punches and Emily falling unconscious. She gave him a run for his money, and he liked it.

They were friends, and then they were lovers. They ate Russian food and fought in the daytime, and at night, they ran on the track on the property. He made love to her in the shower, her back against the hard tile and his strong arms holding her up, whispering nothings in her ear. Sergei knew that Emily would never love him like she once loved Brendan, but he didn't care. Love, no matter its volume, was enough.

Eventually Emily learned to accept that her love for Brendan was past-tense and always would be. Through meditation and gentle coaxes from Sergei, her mind brightened enough to bring to the surface the actual memory of that night, and she had slowly let Brendan go. Brendan would have done anything to help Emily achieve happiness, which is probably why he did what he did that night—held Karla down while Emily gave the last, murderous blow—but he'd gone too far. It wasn't his place to decide to help her kill someone. Even though Emily always knew Brendan would protect her before anyone else, would look out for her and do what was best for her if given the opportunity, it didn't matter. He had gone too far. Because of Emily, he had blood on his hands, and he should have walked away. Emily wasn't mad at him; didn't hate him, but it was easier to blame him than to blame herself, so she did, and her once-romance with Brendan was so far away from her, she didn't believe that she would ever get it back. Not that she wanted to. Her relationship with Sergei, the fucking Russian mobster, was healthier than her relationship with Brendan Tanner had ever been. Brendan had consumed her and, for the first time in her life, she just wanted to exist as Emily. She wanted to be loved, but she didn't want to disappear behind the essence of someone else. Two people in love could stand side by side and still exist independently, and Emily wanted that. She had that, and she wasn't letting it go.

Against his own protest against any kind of slavery—even labor slavery—Sergei bought Emily *Nikes* when her feet started to hurt. Lydia, who was not a redhead, it turned out, cooked dinner and cleaned Emily's blood from the floor of the room of weapons. Sergei taught Emily how to fight with a sword, with a knife, and with her bare hands.

Schizophrenia waned again, albeit by the hands of a different beast. Instead of bliss pushing it away, it was anger. Sergei taught Emily how to fuel her anger through her hands in an effort to keep it from her heart. He never mentioned her mother's death again, and neither did she.

"You are sad," he said to her one night as they lay in bed, stroking her cheek with the back of his rough fingers. She was naked, but he only touched her cheeks; his eyes never left hers. He was such a strange man. "What's wrong?"

"Nothing," she smiled. "Nothing's wrong, Сергей." Her pronunciation of the word was perfect. In time she also learned Russian, though they typically spoke English.

"What?" he persisted. "What do you want? What is missing?"

She kissed him. "Books," she whispered. "I want books."

"You have books," he said, perplexed. "The library downstairs, you have been there, Emily."

"Those are old. And dusty. And . . . Russian. No more Tolstoy, Sergei. I want real books."

He smiled, laughing a little. "You want American books. Like, what? *Fifty Shades of Grey?*"

"Don't insult me," she snarled. "I have already read that one, and it was fucking terrible."

He laughed his deep, boisterous laugh then, the one only she got to hear. "I will get you books," he said. "I will get you all the books in the world."

*   *   *

Six months after Emily had left herself for dead on a Russian bridge, she stared at Sergei as he laced his boots to go out with his team of revolutionaries. He paused, drinking in her half naked body lying on their bed.

"What?" he asked gently, gliding over to her. He kissed the small of her back, gliding his tongue over the edge of her spine. "Tell me what you want," he whispered.

She indulged in the pleasure he afforded her for a moment before she was willing to break it. She wondered how long she could take it. Probably all the way, but she wasn't sure if there was time for that.

"Let me go with you," she said eventually. It was the first time she had ever asked in the months she had watched him leave her on occasional evenings.

His lips paused on her neck, and his bite was ever so light. "Okay," Sergei agreed into her ear, and she was not surprised by his lack of hesitation let alone disagreement. He did not spend half a year's time beating the shit out of the woman he loved for nothing. He respected her as a human being, not just a body with tits and an ass. Having spent her entire life in what was considered the freest country in the world, she had never been treated so equally with so much respect, even with a man's hand on her ass.

Emily would miss Sergei.

*   *   *

In the dark, Moscow looked like an orange and blue *Disneyland*. Headlights pulled the sparkle of the stars in the sky down to the streets, and between the high rises and what Emily identified with as the Cinderella towers, which were actually churches, it was difficult to see anything but the glow of Moscow life. Sergei drove calmly through the streets of the city, and Emily held a gentle piece of black cotton in her hand from the passenger seat. It was not long before they abandoned the bright city for dark alleys and back streets embellished with rough graffiti. Sergei stopped the car just beyond a short tunnel, behind another silver BMW.

"Put it on," he said, gesturing to the piece of cotton fabric in her lap as he shut off the car.

In the trunk were a few knives and swords, but Sergei said they wouldn't need them tonight. It was a somewhat small operation on the grand scale of things, and he hadn't expected to run into any trouble. During one of their morning conversations, Sergei had explained that guns were too loud and brought too much attention to the small group that was his operation. If they ran into someone on one of their runs, they had to kill them quietly and quickly. Silencer or not, the warehouses that the women were typically stored in echoed sound, and when fighting his own people if it came down to it, Sergei couldn't afford any sound.

Quietly, Sergei's voice emerged somewhere from under his mask. "Онаотвечает." *She is in charge.*

Emily resisted the urge to look at Sergei's blue eyes then. That was definitely not something they had discussed, but undermining his authority just by looking at him was the wrong thing to do here.

"Дахорошо," the men simultaneously agreed, and Sergei and Emily led the way down the block. On the street beside them, a semi-truck slowly followed them, driven by another masked man.

The rear entrance to the warehouse looked like any shipping dock in America, except Emily never had any reason to visit any warehouses in Hale or anywhere else in California in the dark. On the small ledge protruding from one of the steel doors, just small enough for a quarter to sit, Sergei balanced on his toes and used a pair of bolt cutters to crack open a rather large lock as if it were a dull nutshell. Emily had imagined that Sergei had his ninja-minions do all the heavy lifting for him, but clearly that was not the case.

"I lift this door," Sergei said in English, as way of offering Emily the option of backing out, "and we will have no more than ten minutes to get in and get out. There will be no alarm, but they will come."

"Откройте дверь, Сергей," Emily said impatiently. *Open the door, Sergei.*

Sergei looked over Emily's head at his team, nodded, and lifted the door.

Before it had reached the top of the structure, Emily placed one pale hand against the cement floor of the warehouse and used the momentum of her legs to fly inside. Tearing the bolt cutters from Sergei's hand, she charged at a long red shipping container against the left wall, basking in her every surrounding while focusing on that single prize. She cut the lock in one swift motion and used all her strength to throw open the door.

When Emily imagined this moment, she anticipated screams or some sort of noise, some sort of sign indicating life inside, but she heard nothing. Again, they couldn't afford sound.

She saw eyes. She saw two-hundred eyes, at least, and only smelled the fear sifting out of the container in waves. But not a sound embellished the warehouse.

Against Sergei's every rule, she tore down her mask. She did not remove it, but only pulled it down to her chin for no more than two seconds. She needed the girls to see that she was a woman. "прийдите быстро!" Emily commanded and she stepped back, Sergei and his men behind her moving to the side to create a tunnel of safety for the girls. *Come quickly!*

She had all five men in her sights, yet there was a faint breath behind her. Bolt cutters still in hand, Emily whirled around, each strand of her hair cutting through the air behind her. In the split second before she swung, a tiny camera lens caught her eyes in its light. The mysterious intruder went down like a sack of bricks as the bolt cutters cracked against the side of his head, and his skull bounced off the concrete. Emily brought her foot down on the smartphone that was in the man's hand, crushing it. Ignoring Sergei's look of horror—or awe, she wasn't sure— Emily repeated her command at the girls. "прийдите быстро!!"

Their skin blackened, like sheep dipped in soot—or maybe it was bruises—the girls slowly filed out of the container. Sergei and his men helped them down the dock, and Emily guided them up the ramp to the semi waiting. She secured it simultaneously as the semi began to roll away, and Emily and Sergei's team—Emily and Emily's team—ran.

They left the man she had just assaulted with a pair of bolt cutters to die. Not that he wasn't already dead.

*   *   *

Regardless of Sergei's wishes, it had been Emily's plan to hop in the truck with the driver to see the operation through. Sergei no longer saw it through until the end as it caused him pain relating to the death of his sister. But the women needed to be cleaned up, fed, nurtured back to health, and shipped out of Russia, and Emily intended to indulge in that experience. But she had killed someone, *again*, and all she could think to do was run at Sergei's side.

She wondered if that made her a serial killer. Probably. She only killed bad people, though. There was at least one book or one movie about that. At least she didn't eat them.

She was surprised to find herself not shaken up on the car ride home. She would have expected the voices to arrive in such a stressful situation, but they didn't. No more than usual since she had been in Russia, that is. Sergei didn't say anything. She took that as, instinctively as she had acted without thinking, she had done the right thing. That is to say, she did what Sergei would have done, had he been standing where she was. She didn't ask who the man with the camera phone could have been. If Sergei knew, they wouldn't have been there. It would just frustrate him further that he couldn't answer her questions.

When they arrived home, Emily showered, deliberately scrubbing the unknown man's blood from her forehead, and she slept in Sergei's arms. She was surprised to find herself alone when she awoke; soon learning that it was into the hours of the next day's sunset.

She got up and got dressed. She turned to the doorway of their bedroom at the sound of Sergei's voice.

"You have to leave," he said.

What? She walked towards him, sliding her hand in his. Sergei, she whispered, I'm sorry, I didn't—I did what I thought—

Emily, stop. You didn't do anything wrong. His face was drained of his own energy and any color that indicated life. The camera, it was feeding . . . somewhere . . . America, I think. The footage shows us all. They will come for me.

In masks only, Sergei. Come with me. She swept her fingertips across his cheek.

I cannot. You will die, and I will never forgive myself. Not even in death.

Emily didn't know what to say.

You cannot take any of my cars, Emily. You have to run. You have to go now.

She let him wrap her in him. He kissed her head and told her that he loved her.

And she ran.

CHAPTER NINETEEN

EMILY'S *NIKES* THUMPED AGAINST the pavement as she weaved through small streets and back alleys, like Sergei had taught her if this situation were ever to occur, which it was, right now. She hopped from a tunnel to the main bridge where she had lost herself her first day in Moscow, just steps from the airport. Stealing a glance behind her, she smacked into something hard, her cheek bouncing off of the surface.

It was a chest.

He caught her before she fell.

In the very moment that she looked up, her knees gave as her very essence melted into mush. She saw a reflection of her violet eyes in the teal orbs directly in front of her face.

Will?! She cried out, gaining her composure on the physical end of things, at least. Will, what the f—

We have to go, Em. We have to go right now.

She inhaled a deep swell of air, letting it collapse between her lips. Where?

Home. I'm taking you home.

Before they boarded the plane, Sergei Melikov would be lying in a pool of his own blood in the bed where he had made love to Emily. The crime photos later leaked to the press would show him on the side where Emily had slept on more nights than she could remember, with his head buried in her pillow.

*   *   *

Flights from Europe weren't exactly short, and Will talked through most of it, while Emily laid her head in his lap. He played with her hair.

The camera was in fact feeding to a major US network. The man was a conflict journalist and had been investigating the anonymous renegades who had been setting the slaves free as of late. He followed a lead to a known member of the Russian mafia—the crime boss's son—Sergei Melikov. The man had followed Sergei and Emily to the warehouse and had never left. The woman with the violet eyes was caught on camera with a pair of bolt cutters for a weapon just before the feed went dead, but that's all anyone had, including Will. A woman with violet eyes. It made sense. He had seen her read that stupid book so many times, but he didn't put it together until then: where she possibly could have disappeared to. He caught the next flight out. He didn't exactly know where he was going once he arrived in Moscow, but it turned out that he didn't need to know.

It was a rare trait, the eyes, but not rare enough. Will assured Emily that her grandparents' ties to the community before they had passed would exonerate her from the remaining crime she had committed nearly a year prior in addition to this one. Will explained that he and Jace had answered the questions the police had about Emily where it related to Karla's death, that her disappearance had been fabricated into a permanent stay at a private institution for the mentally ill by a private investigator—the documentation dated long before Karla had been beaten to death in front of Emily's house—and that any further inquiries would need to be directed to Jace's attorney. There was a funeral, and what happened that night was concluded by local authorities to be a product of a drug deal gone terribly awry. A cold case that would likely never be solved.

Will had covered all the bases, but Emily still didn't believe him.

Mia had died in a car accident at the hands of her husband, who was driving drunk. She was six months pregnant.

And the bookstore was thriving. Savannah continued to follow the model Emily had devised for her business in the months before her brother's death. Savannah had even been updating Emily's book blog.

Will never mentioned Brendan or the band, and she didn't ask.

Emily slept in Will's bed when they got back to Hale, and he took the couch. She expected a culture shock when she returned home, but stepping on American soil was easy. The scent of grass in the sunshine reeked of home. Russia was never that way for her; it was cold and dark and didn't smell like anything but Sergei. Without him, she was an outsider in Moscow, a tourist, and she always would be.

Will drove Emily to the shop a few minutes after nine o'clock in the morning; she hadn't driven in eight months and wasn't prepared to put her Subaru (which Will kept in mint condition, along with her house) in danger just yet. The shop, aside from the books, still smelled like lavender, as if the scent of Emily's soul had lingered all this time. It looked exactly the same. Savannah hadn't changed a thing.

Emily caught sight of her friend in the area where they kept the Fiction/Literature. She dropped the copy of *The Russian Concubine* as she looked up. It took her a moment to react, but her inevitable reaction was so . . . Savannah.

Emily?! Emily! Savannah ran into Emily's arms, nearly knocking her over. Her tears made a swimming pool on Emily's shoulder.

I'm so sorry, Savannah, Emily breathed.

It's— Savannah held Emily's face in her hand. You have nothing to be sorry about. Oh my god, Emily. Are you okay?

Yes, she said, nodding with a half-smile. I'm better now.

Do you want to talk about it?

Not really.

Okay, she hugged her again.

Have you read that book? The one you were looking at just now? No? Is it good?

Yeah, Emily smiled, leading her back over. You know, ever since I read that book, I've always wanted to go to Moscow.

*   *   *

Will made the offer to Emily to stay with him permanently. The other bedroom had been empty since Brendan had moved out two Christmases before. She still didn't know why he had moved out other than the fact that Brendan was Brendan and Will was Will, which was probably exactly why.

Emily respectfully declined. As much as she would enjoy hanging out with Will for the rest of her days, that could get complicated very quickly, and she had some discovery to be made before she hopped into yet another relationship that wouldn't last. He helped her get settled back into her house and promised that he would be available to her whenever she needed him. Emily thanked him gracefully but never called him. He had done enough.

* * *

Emily's door knocked. Or, rather, someone knocked on Emily's door. She pressed the button on the side of her new phone, illuminating the giant screen. It was after two in the morning, and phones were big now.

She looked around at the belongings that seemed to be the epitome of some distant life, as if they didn't belong to her. She had returned home just three days before. She hadn't seen him in so long, and currently, she, and her entire life, was a mess.

He knocked again.

Once upon a time, she would have run to the closest mirror to ensure her appearance was appropriate. Appropriate meaning perfect.

The ideal of external perfection seemed so mundane to her now.

She opened the door.

He charged at her, squeezing her hips so hard that, as he kissed her, she knew they would eventually bruise.

Emily liked it. He knew that.

His hand glided around to the small of her back, sailing up her spine, his fingernails painting trails of red through her shirt onto her pale skin. He seized the back of her neck while his other hand cupped her ass, lifting her against the back of the front door. The weight of his contoured body held her there while he unbuttoned his jeans. With the tips of her toes, Emily reached up to his waist and pushed his pants down to his ankles. He clenched the edge of her dress between his callused fingertips, lifting it up and pushing her cotton underwear to the side. He entered her imprudently, without caution.

She gasped, and a breath escaped his wickedly erotic smile.

He slowed, and her warmth began to drip down his legs. He paused.

Emily didn't look deep into his eyes or any stupid, epical gesture of humanity-defining love, or anything like that. It was all bullshit: true love, soul mates, all of it. You fall in love and you fall out of love and you fall in love again. A hundred times over the course of your lifetime. Humans were never meant to be with just one person. Unless you were Adam and Eve. Which was bullshit too, obviously.

She just waited.

His hand slipped under the back of her dress and he unclutched her bra with two fingers. They always used to joke about his experience with bras. If he couldn't get it unhooked in two seconds or less, it was defective.

The upper portion of Emily's skull echoed as it popped against the back of the door. Her right nipple was between his thumb and forefinger. The sensation bordered between euphoric and unbearable as he squeezed, while jamming his stiffness inside her. Her legs began to tremble as he slowed to a melodic rhythm. He clutched her thighs and wrapped them around his waist. The trembling stopped only for a moment, until he wrapped his fingers around her neck, hard enough to invoke a reaction, but not so that he would leave a mark. He squeezed, and his hand trailed down her chest—painting lines that matched the ones on her back—over her flat stomach, stopping just short of the spot that connected them at present. He kissed her neck, biting down ever so gently. He just wasn't that guy. He'd never leave a mark where it could be seen. He didn't need to mark his territory like a fucking dog.

Emily's breath stuck in her chest as the warmth between her legs caught on fire.

You missed me, he whispered, his words barely comprehensible to her.

Please be quiet, Emily said.

Okay, he said.

Emily's spine dug into the door. His presence drowned her: her nipples were tender, her thighs the shade of yellow that preemptively indicated bruising. Her skin bore the lines of a sketch artist's canvas. He was everywhere.

Yes, he groaned. *Yes.*

Emily used to scream in bed with men and with him, at first. Like a stupid little girl.

Now, Emily didn't make a sound. There was something more defining about the soundless reality that condemned the paradigm of passion. Only the thick scent of breathless sex filled her house.

He collapsed to his knees, the strength of his upper body bringing her down with him, and her eagerness pushed him backwards so he lay on his back on the carpeted floor. She pressed her palms onto his hairy chest and, disregarding whatever it was that he may or may not have wanted, Emily made her own music with their rhythm, releasing the rapture of her being so many times that it spilled down his sides and onto the plush below. Effortlessly, he lifted her from him as he finished and his own bound with hers as it rained down onto his skin.

He looked at her in that way. That way that, when Emily used to look back at the memory of it, she would cry. The same memory that made her smile now.

It was like that the next four times they found themselves entangled in one another before noon the next day, in between shifts of half-dreamt sleep.

It was always like that.

But that was just Brendan and Emily. Two people who simultaneously loved one another too much and not enough.

Insanity is defined by repeating the same act while expecting a different result.

Schizophrenia made insanity easy on Emily, though. Love is like a shadow. You see it right in front of your eyes, but it isn't really there.

Is it?

She looked around at the home that had been hers for years and let her throat attempt to suck down the lump that was stuck in it. The pipe dream that had been her future hours before was just that. Her heart began to pound as shadows enveloped her existence.

She couldn't stay here. She'd be in prison in an hour.

There was only one place she had left to go where she wouldn't disappear forever. If she was completely honest with herself, there was no other place she would rather be, anyway. Now, or ever.

CHAPTER TWENTY

DO YOU HAVE A BOYFRIEND these days?

Savannah looked up as Emily rushed into the store, looking flustered and speaking more quickly than she had ever heard Emily express herself.

Um. No?

Emily roughly swiped her hand across the left side of her face, pushing aside the hair that was attached to the sweat on her forehead. She was wearing a tracksuit and *Nikes* — an outfit the likes of which Savannah had never seen covering Emily's body.

I need to know if you have anything tying you to Hale, Savannah.

Emily knew Savannah was adopted and that aside from Emily and the bookstore, they were all she had here. But Savannah had spent plenty of time with her parents, and whatever this was, they would understand.

She knew better than to press Emily for an explanation of her reasoning for asking such questions. She would clue her in in her own way. Emily had always been that way. Everything in her world existed in her head and wouldn't come out until she was ready to release it.

No, she said finally, I don't.

I want to move the store up north. Emily looked down at the floor as if it would afford her the opportunity to organize her words. But I can't do it without you, Sav.

Emily's fierce violet eyes bled with her own difficulty with expression that she was currently tortured by. Sincere expression had never been her primary strength, and it went without saying that Emily didn't need anyone's help. Everything she had made happen in her twenty-nine-year-old life was on her own.

But Emily needed someone's help now, apparently.

When do we leave, Em?
Now. We leave right now.

*   *   *

Emily didn't say goodbye to Will. Or Brendan, for that matter.

She hired several services to pack up and ship the bookstore and to sell her house and what was in it. She used the same private investigator Will and Brendan had hired once upon a time to get the address she needed in Seattle. She only knew that because she had seen him around at *Shore*.

Savannah promised to meet her after she said goodbye to her parents and tied up her own loose ends. Emily road-tripped it for nearly two days, refueling with punk music and gas station brownies. Emily could have sold the Subaru too, but she didn't have the heart to do it. She loved that fucking car.

Upon arrival, Emily, as the gray sky cried its tears on the most depressed city in the world, made the distinction that it looked to be an outdated, less aesthetically pleasing version of Moscow. The buildings were tall yet square, and its essence was lightless. To Emily, though, it was beautiful in its own idiosyncratic way. It smelled like it could be home.

She did as the robotic voice coming from her navigation system asked and found herself parked in front of a turquoise-ish house with a loft, the amber color of warmth glowing from its many windows.

Emily wasn't even out of the car when he came running out into the rain. He was tall, with a hipster attitude for clothing. He was without shoes, the small black strands of longish hair sticking out from his red beanie catching droplets of rain from above. Emily rushed out of the car and crashed into him in the front yard. He lifted her off the ground, spinning her in circles. Emily didn't cry when she reunited with Savannah, but she cried now. She was crying, and he was crying, and the sky was crying, and it was perfect.

He didn't set her down. I would beat the shit out of you if I wasn't so happy to see you. He kissed her forehead, wrapping his arm tightly around her head. Don't ever fucking do that to me again.

She slipped her arms around his waist and held on tight to his neck. Over his shoulder, a handsome man Emily didn't recognize emerged from the front door. He smiled at her.

Jace, who's your friend?

*   *   *

The interior of the large house was what Emily's life should have looked like since the very moment she had made the sacred pact on the phone to move into this one. Every wall was lined with shelves that housed an unsystematic variation of paperbacks, art, and comic books. The hardwood floors would hurt Emily's bare feet, and she reminded herself to invest in some slippers, as if that was important at the moment. Her room—fully furnished—was half-office/half-bedroom, with a bed fit for one but comfortable for two and a tall oak desk fully set up with a computer. The walls were covered with, not books, but empty white canvases. Emily had once told Jace that she wanted to try to paint.

We'll have to get Savannah all set up when she gets here, Jace's voice said from behind her as she breathed in her new home. The fourth room is completely empty.

Emily hadn't said a word about Savannah being on her way. She looked back at him, smiling gently.

I'll have Loren start looking for a new location for *Danielle's* tomorrow, he said. His parents are in the real estate business.

Emily had learned that Loren was Jace's roommate, who he'd acquired when the author business had failed to pay the bills. Jace's stories were some of Emily's favorites, and that wasn't because he was Jace. He had a way with words, so to speak.

I think I'd like to change the name, Emily said. *Danielle's Books* was the name of the place when she purchased it, and she had never bothered to change it.

To what?

Astral Books, maybe, Emily said.

Jace nodded. I like it.

Emily plopped herself on her blue bed, and Jace lay on the floor next to it. He closed his eyes. Whenever you're ready.

Jace—

Jace lifted his head to look up at her. You may be able to pull that shit with Sav, but not with me. Spill.

Jace apparently had not caught her eyes on the news, probably because he hated the fucking news.

Moscow, Emily said, and she described every detail that was her life since she left her lifeless mother lying in the middle of the street in Hale, California.

Jace cried, and she made him Russian soup.

*   *   *

Savannah arrived the next day, and they shopped for furniture and pink bedding. It didn't take them long to hold down a location for *Astral Books*. It had a larger open space than *Danielle's* and was big enough to include the coffee shop Jace and Emily had always talked about. After painting it the same neutral scheme as *Danielle's* and moving all of the books and furniture in, they went about a month with barely any customers, which was okay since Emily's house had been sold and she could afford it. Through the book blog that Savannah had kept up for Emily and was still in charge of, they were lucky enough to catch wind of a local author whose novel had just debuted. They deliberately planned an event with French wine and a delectable cake shaped like the Eiffel tower. Loren used his parents' reach to market the event, and the turnout was astronomical. It was that evening that word began to get out about the *Limehouse Coffee Shop,* which was attached to *Astral*. There were more than one-hundred-and-fifty coffee cocktails to try—some containing alcohol—and every single cup served was embellished with the words from a different book. In six months, no two paper cups had been sold with the same passages on them. Under the bulb lamps hanging from the ceiling (also with quotes on them), the books on the oak tables were the only books in the history of coffee houses that were actually read instead of being used just for decoration. They capitalized on the vaping culture that was slowly making its way up the coast, and integrated a vaping bar on the far side of the coffee shop. The friends' business of literature, coffee, and a safer alternative to smoking was the most successful in Seattle in the shortest documented amount of time. They had discussed opening a few more stores, but Jace, Savannah, and Emily had agreed that it would cheapen the art that was their place, and they vowed to embrace it for what it was.

Loren was an acoustic musician, and he played at the store sometimes. Sans Schizophrenia, murder, and the Russian mafia, Emily had built an honest friendship with him. She told him about Brendan and about Frank. Eventually, Loren became interested in Emily romantically. She had thought about it—he was handsome and charming—but distanced herself enough to let it diminish. The more days that passed, the more she missed Will and the rhythm they had been dancing to all these years, just like Frank had pointed out to Brendan. Every time she closed her eyes, instead of the blackness within she saw the crisp color of teal as he held her on the streets of Moscow. She realized much too late that she was in love with him, in such a way that was more defining than she had been with Brendan. Brendan had been a fad; Will was a lifestyle. Even if the realization had hit her during the short albeit valid connection in the minimal post-Russia days in Hale, it still would have been too late. Regardless of what had occurred in the years before she turned thirty, Will was still Brendan's best friend and, even if Emily had all but forgotten about Brendan long ago, she wasn't that kind of woman. She would not be passed around a circle of friends. She had chosen to do what she had done with Brendan for so long, and she had to live with that choice. As time passed, the thought of calling Will ailed her, and she never did. Even without a man to call her own, Emily wasn't alone like she had been most of her life, and so she was never lonely. Just like Savannah had always told her, everything was going to be okay. Everything was okay.

Emily never again achieved the giddy happiness that she once had between pedicures and girls' nights in Hale, and that fact in itself couldn't make her happier. It was wonderful to have experienced a life that was perfect every day, but it wasn't Emily's *life*. It was what Brendan wanted for her, and not necessarily what Emily had wanted. Emily had gone through what she had gone through to achieve neutralism, and there was no epitome of a completely neutral outlook on life as accurate as Emily in her present days. Schizophrenia was there, but not debilitating. She loved, but it did not consume her. Emily Colt existed as no other person could because she was Emily Colt.

In her spare time, she did research on Schizophrenia at a doctorate level. She did appreciate her time with Frank and with Brendan because it prepared her for that and prepared her to learn how to embrace her illness rather than be defined by it. She had good days and bad days, but there wasn't more of one or the other, which afforded her a somewhat normal life with her favorite people in the world in her favorite place in the world.

Life wasn't perfect, but it wasn't supposed to be. Eternal beauty could not exist if it were not for the face of a fatal flaw.

CHAPTER TWENTY-ONE

LOREN STEPPED INTO THE CHAOS that had replaced Emily's room. She was standing in the middle of the room, her gaze switching from one wall to the other and back again. Her canvases were splattered with red and black paint, bleeding over the writing he couldn't read. She had written over every space of the room with a permanent marker. Loren took a step back as Emily began to laugh.

"Emily . . . " he said carefully.

"Loren!" she spun around to look at him. "Look." She pointed at the walls. "Look, they weren't trying to hurt me; they were trying to help me!"

"Emily, you have to calm—"

"No, Loren, don't you understand? Look. He whispered to me as a child because he didn't want to scare me, but I didn't understand him, and as I got older, he raised his voice. It's standard reaction to yell when someone can't hear you, right? He got so frustrated that he turned red. He's only there when I'm stressed or upset." She stepped towards him. "Don't you get it? He was trying to help me through it; he was trying to tell me that everything was going to be okay. He didn't want me to be alone. It's not an illness, Loren, it's a fucking blessing. Some kind of . . . guardian angel . . . or something." She grabbed her marker from the floor and she began to write some more. Loren still couldn't read what any of it said.

He was scared of her, and so he did the only thing he could think one would do when in fear.

He called the police.

*   *   *

Savannah busted through the double doors of the bookstore, calling Jace's name in a breathless panic. Hanging up the phone attached to his ear, Jace held onto her shoulders as words gushed out of Savannah at an indiscernible rate.

"Breathe," Jace said, gently shaking Savannah. "Tell me what happened. Calmly."

"Loren had Emily committed," Savannah said, tears streaming down her face.

"What?!" A fire ignited from somewhere inside Jace, and it scorched his skin.

"There is writing all over the walls—on the canvases, I mean. She figured it out, Jace. She figured everything out and when she tried to explain it to Loren he called the fucking police on her."

"Come on," he said, grabbing her hand and dragging her out of the store and yelling to one of their employees about an emergency.

"How are we going to get her out, Jace?" Savannah asked frantically, running beside him on the way to his car.

"I'll get her out, Sav, *today*," he promised. "Not optional. We have to get her back to Hale. Right now."

"What? Why?"

"Get in the car and I'll explain on the way."

*   *   *

"She has Paranoid Schizophrenia," an older man in a white coat said quietly to Loren, in a white hallway with white linoleum.

"That's *impossible*," Loren argued, based on his experience with the beautiful woman who loved books and fudge brownies.

"It is not," the doctor said adamantly. "Everything she says is a lie that she believes is the truth. The name she called out when you brought her in here? Will? Her oldest friend you told me about, Brendan? They don't exist. We checked. We have dug into Emily's memories and they are all fake. Emily Colt is an orphan and has been her entire life. She doesn't have any siblings and she doesn't speak Russian. Or Dutch,

which she also claims. Please understand that these *people*—schizophrenics—
they live a lie every day. Her past and everyone in it, they are like . . . like
Paper Souls. Being schizophrenic is a lot like being a writer. People don't
exist until she makes them up in her head, and that's where they stay.
It's one revolving hallucination. She hears *voices*, Mr. Walker. Your
friend is psychotic."

Loren took a deep breath. "What can we do for her, doctor?"

"We will keep her until we can medicate her enough to reduce or
eliminate the hallucinations and we can safely release her."

"The fuck you will," Jace's voice roared from behind Loren. His head
snapped around and his eyes found Jace charging towards him. He
followed his first instinct and stepped behind the doctor. Where Emily
was concerned, Jace did not fear imprisonment or death. He feared
nothing. If the doctor wasn't standing in his way, Jace would have
killed him right then and there.

"Cut her loose," he demanded, Savannah silent beside him. "Now."

"I don't know who you think you are," Dr. Boleyn said, "but—"

"I am Emily Colt's Power of Attorney and Health Care Proxy," Jace
matter-of-factly informed him. "She has afforded me every right to make
decisions on her behalf. She did not attempt to hurt herself or anyone
else; she has not broken any laws. If she is not released from the padded
prison you are holding her in to my care in exactly five minutes, my
lawyer and half of Seattle's press will be outside those doors. I will
have you and everyone in this fucking Hall of Death arrested on charges
of false imprisonment and deprivation of liberty."

The doctor crossed his arms, not in the least perturbed by Jace's threats.

"You fucking idiot," Jace spat at the old man. "Does the name Colt
not ring any bells? Let me give you a hint since you are so unbelievably
stupid. Emily Colt, daughter of Ben Colt, son of Deena and George Colt,
the late mayor of a little town in California known as Hale, the same
mayor who raised and donated millions of dollars to this very hospital
for Schizophrenia research. Do you see where this is going, *doctor*?"

The color of the doctor's skin camouflaged into the white walls
surrounding him as the realization drained him of life, and his mouth
gaped open.

"Release her right now, or I swear to god I will take you and this
entire operation down. You will not even have that stupid fucking white
coat to hide under when I'm finished with you."

"Lisa," the doctor called behind him. "Discharge the patient from room one. Now."

*   *   *

Savannah kept Loren company while Jace and Emily sat together on a bench just a few feet outside the hospital doors. She was not nearly as angry with Loren as Jace was; she could not fault him for not knowing any better. No one in the world knew better, really. Savannah assumed that Emily wanted to get off these grounds as soon as possible, but if she knew anything about Jace, she knew nothing or no one could touch her while he was at her side.

"He slit his wrists," she heard Jace say to Emily.

She blinked tears out of her eyes and they streamed down her red cheeks. Her arms were bruised from wrestling with her captors and there were dark rings around her wrists. Her hair was tangled and she was shaking.

"Is he dead?" she asked.

"No. He's in a coma, though."

"Take me to him, Jace."

"I will. Savannah will stay behind to take care of things while we're gone. Loren comes with us until I decide whether or not to let him live."

"Why? Just . . . just let him live his banal life, Jace."

"No. He comes with us, so I can be sure that he never, ever does this to someone again."

*   *   *

How does one begin at a time such as this? Goodbye? I hate you? I'm sorry you found me on the roof lying in a pool of the blood that leaked from the narrow cuts in my wrists that I myself slit; that must have been terrible for you? I don't know. I never planned to write one such as this when I entered this place without a cry—or a worry—in the world.

It's not my parents' fault. This world was far too fucked up when even they got here and, though there was a time I liked to think myself optimistic enough to think otherwise, I'm pretty sure they couldn't have fixed it if they tried. *They could have tried though. It would speak greater for their character if they had done something to try before bringing a child into this world. People think so lightly of children, of life. Let's have a baby! Why? Because you want to give something back that is valid and is important and is beautiful to your world that gave so much to you? Yeah, that too, but I really just want a kid. You . . . want a kid. For what reason? Oh . . . I don't know . . . I've always wanted to be a mother...*

. . . You are the stupidest fucking person I have ever met.

I had a friend like that once. Had a child young because she wanted one. No accident about it. Of course, the next four were accidents. Who knows who the fathers were or are or if they themselves even know they have children. I doubt it, considering she is now broke, with a hatred for her children that my father only reserves for flies. (He keeps bug poison on the nightstand by his bed.) Which, broke, being broke isn't so bad. It's kind of awesome, actually. No one pays any attention to the broke people, especially the government. But hating your children for . . . what? Ruining your social life? Your sex life? How about that time you ruined five human being's lives for your own selfish purposes? I don't even know if that is why you did what you did. Do you have purpose? What is your purpose for bearing five children by five different men? When it comes down to it, I don't know what's worse. Giving your children up to this run-down foster system that is no functional system at all, or stealing from your children the only chance they have at a fair shot at life. I guess they are pretty much the same thing.

I would have been a good father, a real father, if this world hadn't stolen my son from me. If the very plague I'm running away from hadn't killed him.

That is the absolute reason I am writing this, isn't it? The reason that tonight, when The Sandman refuses to visit me like he did when I was young, I will do what I will do? They will think I was unhappy. You will think I was unhappy. You will be wrong. Even he, who loves to pretend that he knows me, will be wrong. I am happy, or could have been. If everyone would have left me the fuck alone. That was really all I wanted. And I imagine that, had I had five children, I would want them to leave me the fuck alone, too.

That is, of course, until I didn't want to be left alone anymore. But when the world gave me another chance at life, I failed it. I failed her, and she is gone. Everything is gone.

So I shall say goodbye. Farewell to every person who only pretended to care, and . . .

And . . .
to the only person who ever did.
Shit.

In the darkness, Brendan looked up from the note. He looked for hope in his unconscious best friend who was beeping at him from a hospital bed across the room. Will's wrists were wrapped in gauze that was once white but now was dyed in his own blood. Brendan gulped down the threat of bile. This place smelled of ammonia and death.

Brendan eventually fell asleep, waking after an indeterminable amount of time to the incessant beeping. Coming to, he found Emily standing in the doorway.

"Oh, thank god," Brendan whispered, mostly to himself.

Emily ignored him, slowly tiptoeing over to the bed. Brendan got up and brought his chair to her. She sat down, and he gave her space as Jace and a man he'd never seen before walked in.

"Where's Savannah?" he asked quietly.

"Home," Jace said, more coldly than he needed to. "Overseeing business affairs."

Brendan nodded, focusing his attention on Emily. She reached under the hospital sheets and pulled Will's arm out. She linked her hand into his and laid her cheek upon his chest.

"Open your eyes," she said.

And Will, he did not open his eyes. He did open his mouth, though. To Brendan, he said, "I am going to fucking kill you."

The world was sucked out of the hospital room and not one soul made a sound. No one breathed, except Emily. She said it again. "Open your eyes."

That time he did, and as quickly as his eyelids popped open, they closed again, to allow his own tears to fall. "Emily," he gasped, and he began to hyperventilate. "Emily, I'm sorry, I'm so sorry." He grabbed her by the waist and pulled her to him, crying into her hair.

She slipped under the sheets with him, laying her head on his shoulder. "Don't you ever try to leave me again," she said.

"You left me," he pointed out. "Twice."

She got up from the bed, walked out of the hospital room doorway, and returned two seconds later. She resumed her spot beside him, covering herself with the sheets, and she said, "And I came back. Twice," she said.

Will laughed, and the whole world breathed again.

EPILOGUE

"WHO ARE THESE PEOPLE?" Loren asked Jace in a whisper.

Jace looked from Loren to the occupied hospital bed. "Do you notice how the sane person has been committed due to a suicide attempt, and the *psychotic* girl is the one saving him?"

Loren looked down at the floor without a reply.

"That," Jace said, pointing at the dark-haired man in the bed, "is William Young, the man who saved Emily from the mafia in Russia. Her Russian is stellar, by the way. So is her Dutch. You know why? Because she is fucking Dutch. And that," Jace said, looking at the sleeping man curled up in a chair like a kitten, "is Brendan Tanner. You know, just a couple people that only exist in Emily's head. Maybe we're all hallucinating."

Jace's eyes were fierce, cutting through the darkness as he glared at Loren. "You see, Emily Colt isn't crazy. And if you ever threaten her life again like you did today, I'll fucking kill you."

THE END

ALSO BY ALLIE BURKE

Violet Midnight (Paranormal Romance) A powerful enchantress meets a handsome man with a painful past, and so begins a love story that will change the world as they know it, forever.

Emerald Destiny (Paranormal Romance) Young, handsome Evan has loved forbidden Abby since childhood, but is his passion strong enough to overcome the forces working to keep them apart.

Amber Passion (Paranormal Romance) Can the enchanting Claire soothe Daniel's darkness as he yearns for her without even realizing it as he mourns a separation from his twin sister?

The Enchanters Collection (Paranormal Romance Collection) This genre-defining trilogy weaves the beautiful complexity of true love through auras, darkness, and magic.

MORE GREAT READS FROM BOOKTROPE

Living and Dying with Dogs **by Duke Miller** (Literary Fiction) Living and Dying with Dogs is a journey from war to epidemic to famine. Your tour guide? A hesitant, unsure narrator with a unique and tragic understanding of refugees, war, sex, the past, and our bloody world.

Vacation **by JC Miller** (Literary Fiction) Haunted by his wife's senseless murder, a reluctant traveler confronts his past in this story of love, loss and forgiveness.

Discover more books and learn about our new approach to publishing at **booktrope.com**

17236425R00077

Made in the USA
Middletown, DE
13 January 2015